For
Sharon Weiss,
Bryan Leys,
Frann Gersh,
Wes Gersh,
Max Gersh,
Lizzie Gersh,
Eileen Weiss,
and
Michael Weiss

DREAMS
AND
VISIONS

FOURTEEN FLIGHTS OF FANTASY

EDITED BY

M. JERRY WEISS AND
HELEN S. WEISS

A TOM DOHERTY ASSOCIATES BOOK • NEW YORK

DREAMS AND VISIONS: FOURTEEN FLIGHTS OF FANTASY

Copyright © 2006 by M. Jerry Weiss and Helen S. Weiss

This book is printed on acid-free paper.

A Starscape Book
Published by Tom Doherty Associates, LLC
175 Fifth Avenue
New York, NY 10010

www.starscapebooks.com

Library of Congress Cataloging-in-Publication Data

Dreams and visions : fourteen flights of fantasy / [compiled by] M. Jerry Weiss and
Helen S. Weiss.—1st ed.
p. cm.
"A Tom Doherty Associates book."
ISBN: 0-765-31249-2
EAN: 978-0-765-31249-5
1. Fantasy.   2. Young adult fiction. [1. Fantasy.   2. Short stories.]   I. Weiss, M. Jerry
II. Helen S. Weiss.
PZ5.D74857 2006
[Fic]—dc22   2005016724

First Edition: April 2006

Printed in the United States of America

0   9   8   7   6   5   4   3   2   1

CONTENTS

ACKNOWLEDGMENTS

Susan Chang and Kathleen Doherty at Tor Books for their help and encouragement.

Eileen Weiss for her assistance with this manuscript.

INTRODUCTION

When we first heard the magical words "once upon a time," our imaginations took flight. We discovered the wonders, visions, dreams, escapades of so many characters in stories. Finding the lass who lost her glass slipper, watching a beautiful girl kissing a frog and hearing about the frog turning into a handsome prince, reading about Pinocchio, Peter Pan and Tinkerbell, Merlin, Harry Potter, Artemis Fowl, Charlie Bone, the amazing Maurice, Eragon, and many more, showed us the power of story and imagination.

We followed those who adventured to Oz, Middle-Earth, Lilliput, and met little people, elves, giants, hobbits, witches, wizards, monsters, dragons, and a variety of creatures that filled our brains. Oh, we soared through time and space, saw miracles, witnessed battles, and had visions and dreams that filled our faraway thoughts. Was any of this possible?

In science fiction and fantasy imagination rules. Einstein once said, "Imagination is more important than knowledge." He knew that without visions and dreams, with time limitations in our thoughts, we would hardly think about the future. Science and technology in some stories raise questions about what might be. *Ender's Game* by Orson Scott Card, *The War of the World* by H. G. Wells, *20,000 Leagues Under the Sea* by Jules

Verne shake us up as we realize the time in which they were written and what has happened in a Star Wars universe. Thank goodness for heroes and heroines with knowledge and powers to keep humanity safe from aliens, dragons, ghosts, and other possible evil forces.

In this volume, we see outstanding young-adult writers travel near and far as they use their talents to create more tales to enthrall. In "Blocked," Joan Bauer tells us about Chloe, a fantasy writer who is trying to write a new story. She has numerous false starts with different settings, characters, creatures. But what would be different or new?

Suzanne Fisher Staples introduces us to the powers of djinn and how fates can be dictated in this story that follows the death of a leader and beloved grandfather. The story takes place in Pakistan.

Charles de Lint provides a romance in "Dharma." But Dharma wants to know so much: who is the girl? Where is she? The vision is very real. But what about that night?

Michael O. Tunnell creates a murder mystery as onlookers watch the burial of Beratha by her son, Martin. The town knew she was a witch, but on many an occasion she had done good. Who would have killed her? Why? When Beratha's vision comes to Martin, urging him to seek revenge, what choices does he have?

Rich Wallace shows us two young people, Jessica and Craig, who are on a track team and love to run. They were strangers at first; but were they? Could this be a story of a transformation? Is Craig reminiscing about another existence?

Patrice Kindl brings an elderly woman, Mrs. Duck, to live

in a section of town, Refreshing Acres. She seems so friendly and kind. She offers sweets to children and even a few adults. She even offers to babysit. But who is she really? What does she want?

In S. L. Rottman's story, the world is on fire. Only Hybream and Kief make it to the water's edge. Kief knows he can't swim, but he must jump in or be burned as the rest were. But what about Hybream? Where was she? Who was she?

David Lubar's story setting was the junior contest for the North American Magicians' Association. Deborah, who is thirteen, knows she must win this contest. But there's a young brat who might charm the judges because of his age. He keeps calling, "Girls can't be magicians!" But can't they? Even girls have dreams and visions. . . .

Mel Glenn, in poetic form, shares a conversation between Ryan and an angel. Ryan, after being in a terrible accident, lies in a hospital bed awaiting a most serious decision. Will he live or die? What does fate have in store for him?

An old woman, Warty, in Nancy Springer's story, tells Jessie to pay attention as the class is reading *As You Like It*. Jessie, as she views her dysfunctional family, has her doubts about Warty's advice. Then a toad appears. . . .

John H. Ritter's ghost tale is set after the death of a soldier and his meeting with T. J. McVeigh, remembered for the Oklahoma bombing. War is hell. The conversation between these two reveals the traumas and aftereffects brought about by wars, killings, and so much blood and death.

In Sharon Dennis Wyeth's tale, an oracle makes a prediction. What does it mean? After Celeste's father dies, Celeste and her mother have a difficult life. What is to become of them? What about the prediction? Will it have any meaning in their lives?

Neal Shusterman introduces us to a young thief who holds the fate of the universe in his hand. As the author leads us back and forth and shows us the inquisitor who is testing the young thief, what will be the outcome?

Tamora Pierce's story carries us to Hartunjur, where priests viewed veiled women as subservient to men. If women are caught out of line, such as being taught to read and learn for themselves, they can be severely punished or put to death. But are changes possible? What does the oracle say? What about the Book of Distaff or the Book of the Sword?

Stories of science fiction and fantasy are ambiguous. There are many dreams and visions. What really is happening? Readers often have to draw their own conclusions or just keep wondering. They have to think.

—M. JERRY WEISS AND HELEN S. WEISS

DREAMS
AND
VISIONS

BLOCKED

{ JOAN BAUER }

Chloe, the author in this story, is bogged down by writer's block. She has lost her words. But just as she is about to give up all hope, her computer mysteriously beeps and blinks. Her characters kick in and come to her rescue. With humor and irony, Bauer takes us through a writer's angst until the words come back to her.

The problem is, my princess isn't working.

I've stuck her on a mountain in the middle of winter.

I've shut her up in a cave with greasy, irascible creatures.

I've given her a cool sword to fend off encroaching evil, and I really hate to say it, but she's coming out flat.

Normally, I'd be able to work through this—I've created enough princesses. There was Lady Katarina Wellingcott of the Kingdom of Rottenburg, basically a rotten place to be except for Katarina, who kicked butt and got the lazy royals to start cleaning up the town—caring about things, pulling a vision together, etc. There was Princess Drusilla, my personal favorite, who could ride on a whale's back and turn into a butterfly when needed. Everyone loved her, especially the hunky Ian the Bold, who proposed in twenty-four hours. They lived happily ever after, too, with only a few minor glitches brought on by that dysfunctional dragon, Larry, who kept threatening to set the kingdom on fire at inopportune times. Dragons think the world revolves around them. There isn't time to go into detail about my other princesses who wrestled lions, saved the masses, and used their riches to help the poor—not a damsel-in-distress that couldn't get out of a fantastic fix among them. I am proud of my contributions to the world of fantasy. I am proud to be the coeditor, along with Murray Lowengard, of the first-ever fantasy anthology to be published by my high school writing club, Pen and Ink (a challenging name since we all use computers)—an anthology which we will sell for *money*.

I was sure I could just toss this story off, too, but the fair Princess Adriana of Nottingswood-Glouthshire, is, alas, *boring*.

I don't know why I can't get into her character. It's not like I don't understand her plight. Her father is a demanding king who thinks he's God's gift to the region. This cuts close to home because my father lives to control everyone around him. When it comes to all those toady suitors pledging their devotion, I feel her pain—particularly in the scene with Prince Duller, who bears a distinct resemblance to my last boyfriend, Lewis. She is the middle princess, too, with a crabby older sister and a younger one who is sweet but clueless. It is up to Adriana to keep the peace, handle her father, and be wise beyond her years without seeming overbearing. The Middle Ages was not the most empowering time for women.

I have droopy dialogue to contend with, too, like the exchange in the scene where Adriana has been locked in the dark chamber by the vile reptile, Listernum, who has bad breath that knocks you flat. He is roaring in stark hostility, telling her how he has come to avenge the death of his uncle, who was killed by her father years before when he was out scouting the region for evil. Listernum roars that he is going to kill Adriana by one of three methods. She gets to pick between:

fire
starvation
never sleeping.

This is where a princess's true grit should come out, but all I can think for Adriana to say is: "You'll never get away with this, Listernum. All that is good will save me before all that is evil will engulf me."

And what, really, can a vile reptile say to that, except: "You have chosen your own fate, Princess Adriana. You will die from all three."

So, okay. It's a grim moment. And Listernum goes for high drama as he locks her into the dark chamber and locks door after door behind her as he leaves. But it's early in the story, and with all the buildup I've done, everyone knows that Adriana is going to get out somehow. But no guys move in to save the maiden in my stories. So I'm working on her escape maybe she could have a knife strapped to her leg and she surprises Listernum before he locks her in; maybe the sound of her voice could stop Listernum just long enough for her to escape; maybe she has a magic cape, and when she twirls it, she turns into a bird that can fly away through steel doors. But when a writer resorts to gimmicks, you're basically telling your readers that you don't really know your characters.

I've been wracking my brain. How do I get her out? I've gone back over my notes and thought about who she is. I've asked myself, do I have any interesting back story that could reveal her personality and the core of her strength? I could give her a pet unicorn, but what would *that* do? You can't just hurl mythical beasts around without a good reason.

I ponder this and ponder this.

I consider the basic lesson that all fantasy heroes and heroines ultimately learn.

Believe in yourself.

And when you do, you can:

(a) slay the dragon
(b) drain the pond
(c) ride on the dolphin's back to freedom
(d) climb the mountain
(e) escape from the cave down the long, terror-lined
    hallway past the humorless trolls who don't give a rip
    about personal hygiene.

I look at my mangled story, consider my fast approaching deadline.

I can feel Listernum's beastly breath breathing down my neck.

Believe in yourself, Chloe.

Fat chance.

The truth is . . .

The frightening thing is . . .

I am stuck on this story.

Triple locked in a dark chamber without words.

As blocked as I have ever been.

I call Murray, my trusty coeditor, and announce that I am frozen in literary despair and there is no way out. I apologize profusely for messing up this deadline.

Murray says, "Figure it out, Chloe. You're the first story in the Table of Contents. The promo material is already printed."

"Don't," I protested, "make me the first story!"

"It's too late."

I mention that the first story is the anchor, and this story isn't good enough to be the anchor due to the fact that I am a worm that will probably never finish another short story again, which will cause my hopeful career as a fantasy writer to go down the toilet, which will mean that my hopes and dreams have turned to ashes.

"Give your princess something she needs to overcome personally, Chloe, and have her face her fear. And do it quick."

Well, that's easy for Murray to say. Murray finished his ogre short story last week—not that the ogre was short, he was gargantuan—but it's already been edited by *me*, so Murray can breathe easy. Whereas I am suffocating in a dark and wordless chamber.

No one understands the meaning of lost words like a writer.

I sit there on my bed with my knees bent, staring glumly at my laptop screen, cringing at the ordinariness of this particular exchange on page five when Listernum sends the creature with fourteen eyes into the chamber to check on Adriana. Adriana has met the creature several times before.

CREATURE WITH FOURTEEN EYES: So, Adriana,
  we meet again.
ADRIANA: Guess so.

I, their creator, shout, "There is so much more I want to give you!"

Perhaps it is the literary angst, perhaps it is my need for something to break out, perhaps it is that I've truly lost my grip.

A creepy feeling settles over the room.

My hamster, Cedric, begins running around and around on his wheel with a wild look in his eyes.

The lamp by the bed grows dim.

My computer feels hot.

Then my laptop beeps, beeps again; the tools icon begins to blink, which has never happened before. I sit there staring, feeling that my laptop might suddenly explode. I put the computer down, but a voice says, "Pick it up."

Cedric is running so fast you can only see the blur of his wheel.

"Pick it up!"

The voice seems to be coming from the laptop. It's a man's voice and he is irritated.

I gulp. "What if I don't?"

A sigh from the computer. The voice: "That's not an option. Pick it up and click on the tool bar."

I do.

The screen jumbles with letters and numbers changing quickly to a blur.

On the screen now: a creature with many eyes, a fair maiden, a king with a potbelly, two sisters—one difficult, one sincere; an evil reptile.

These are my characters!

I try to speak, but they beat me to it. They begin talking all at once. I can't understand what they're saying, but they are indignant. And they seem to be indignant at *me*.

"One at a time," I plead.

The king puts his hands on his hips and shouts, *"Silence!"*

That shuts them up, except for the reptile, who breathes heavily.

A royal trumpet sounds. The king steps forward and glares at me. *"What* have you done?"

I close my eyes.

I shake my head to get rid of the images.

Maybe I've been working too hard. . . .

Not getting enough sleep . . .

The king adjusts his crown and stands there waiting.

"What . . . do you mean?" I whisper.

"Why have you left us here?"

I feel defensive for some reason. "I'm trying to, you know, figure out the story."

"What's the holdup, girl?"

At that, the other characters murmur and nod like I've made a wrong turn in traffic and caused an accident.

This can't be happening.

"You guys are just . . ." I struggle for the right words. "You're just a *first draft!*"

"*Insolent subject!*" The king claps his hands twice and the screen goes blank.

I sit there in the encroaching darkness.

"Okay," I say to Cedric. "That didn't just happen. Right?"

Cedric sits motionless on his wheel.

If a raven comes through the window next, I swear, I'm out of here.

There are times when the questions we ask become shouts, not whispers.

I've always liked that line. I wrote it in my last story.

Why have you left us here?

I'm not too crazy about this line.

Did my king really shout it?

Maybe I was dreaming. . . .

Maybe . . .

Why have you left us here?

I think of my characters. The king is so much like my dad— so controlling, unable to listen to reason; his word is law and everyone is supposed to bow down at his feet.

Who is Adriana like? Why isn't she more alive?

I look at my computer on my lap. Did the king break it? I press the on switch. Feel the hum of connection.

The menu pops onto the screen—*Works in Progress* is blinking. I click and face my story and read page one; I've never liked page one.

Inspiration grips me.

I write:

It was the time of unending sorrow in the kingdom for Adriana's mother, the queen, had lost her way, and though they tried to find her, she seemed to be gone forever, lost to only a memory now of golden hair, soft, gentle touches, and a tinkling laugh that always preceded her down the halls of the castle.

Adriana had tried to stop her mother when she went out without her cloak, for the weather was turning so cold. Surely the snow would come as the wise man had predicted. But the queen had a mind of her own and was too fond of summer to ever believe that winter would last for long. Winter did come while she was walking. The snow poured down and the queen could not find the way back to the castle. The swirls of it were so strong, she couldn't see. She grew colder and colder and finally lay down, too weak to fight, too weak to move. They tried to rescue her, but the storm had caused her steps to vanish on the path. The great storm took the queen in its swirling clouds.

It was the beginning of the curse.

And ever since then, snow became a thing to fear for Adriana.

She wondered, as she watched more and more of it fall, if it would come and snatch her away too.

Wow. I am breathing hard after writing that. My mother had died soon after my baby sister was born. It was on the day of a huge winter storm—four feet of snow fell, traffic stalled, and my father couldn't get her to the hospital. An ambulance could have, maybe. But Dad wouldn't hear of that.

Over the years, Adriana ran from snow and wouldn't go out until spring came, but in her she knew that she had to face her fear. The unicorn had told her that.

So, I tell myself, I'll need her journey of escape to be in winter. She'll have to face her fear and it will have to seem like she can't do it, it's too hard.

I remembered hating this house after Mom's funeral. I couldn't live here, I told my father. We have to go someplace warm.

We didn't move. I had to face life here with the memories of my mother.

I look back at the exchange on page five:

CREATURE WITH FOURTEEN EYES: So, Adriana, we meet again.
ADRIANA: Guess so.

How can I deepen it?

CREATURE WITH FOURTEEN EYES: So, Adriana, we meet again, but this time it is snowing.
ADRIANA: Yes, but I am ready.
And she throws a wool cape over her shoulders and runs through the door to freedom.

Too easy.

I try again.

CREATURE: So Adriana, we meet again, except the
snow will do the work for me and keep you captive.
You think you can save your kingdom now? What a
foolish girl you are!

ADRIANA: I am ready to face whatever comes!
What I know to be true is stronger than what I fear.
Move aside, creature. I fear you no more. You cannot
hold me!

She clicks her mountain boots together. The creature is forced to step aside. She throws a wool cape
over her shoulders, and runs through the falling flakes
to save the kingdom.

Not bad.

My tool bar is blinking again.

My hamster is whirling in the wheel.

I breathe deep, click.

The king appears on the screen, looking a bit relieved, but
not by much.

"My character needs deepening," he says.

"*What?*"

"I don't think my true strengths are coming out."

I sit here stunned.

"*Do it,*" he orders.

So I write about how the king mourned and went into his
chamber, which became a place of dark isolation. I write
how all the flowers withered from sadness and the birds

were not allowed to sing, except for one bird who broke the rules and sang a song that lifted the king's spirits.

The king looks at the words I've written and nods.

"I'd like a new wife," he adds.

Some secondary characters just try to take over a story.

"I'm not sure you're ready for that, Your Majesty."

He didn't like that. "There is a point for every fiction writer where one's characters become so real that they tell you what to do. When that happens, you'd bloody well better listen."

So I give him a wife, a thirty-something princess from the next kingdom over who is gentle and funny and kind and brings out the king's heart once again, particularly toward Adriana.

I keep writing. I can't stop.

Listernum is brought to justice. The creature with fourteen eyes turns to stone. The curse on the castle and the kingdom is broken. Adriana saves the day, but it doesn't change her. She becomes wildly famous throughout the region and dozens of interesting suitors come to call, professing deep devotion.

I particularly like this part. I've not had a decent date in months.

I type "The End" and know that it is really finished.

I send it to Murray, who says it's my best one yet. "I knew you could do it, Chloe."

Days pass; normal ones, too. The anthology is printed. The initial sales look strong.

Then Cedric starts running crazily in his wheel.

My computer grows warm, the letters and numbers whirl across the screen.

I take a deep breath. Am I ready for this?

The royal trumpeter announces His Highness.

The king strides across the screen, sits on his throne, and nods to me. "I've been thinking about a sequel," he announces. "Take this down."

And, trust me, I do.

I don't miss a word.

JAMEEL AND THE HOUSE OF DJINN

{ SUZANNE FISHER STAPLES }

When his grandfather suddenly dies, Jameel must leave school in the United States and return to Pakistan, where he faces a difficult decision. Staples uses supernatural incidents to develop the plot, including several episodes involving the mischievous djinn and the recurring appearance of the departed grandfather.

Jimmy was about to kiss a blond girl named Chloe as his beloved grandfather slipped into a coma on the other side of the world. The kiss never happened.

"I've gotta go," Jimmy said, pulling back. He kick-flipped his skateboard and caught it with one hand.

"What?" Chloe said. Her eyes had been closed in anticipation of her first kiss from this handsome, mysterious guy. "What's wrong?"

"I don't know," Jimmy said. A strange prickle had skipped over his shoulder blades, as if someone had tickled him. It was a typical late summer San Francisco day—cool and clear as the sun burned off the fog. "I just had this funny feeling. . . ." Chloe bit her lower lip, trying not to smile.

"Did it ever occur to you," she asked, "that a strange feeling is good when you're about to kiss someone you like?" At that moment Jimmy's cell phone began to vibrate in his pocket. He retrieved it and flipped open the cover in a single, practiced move.

"Yes, Mommy," he said softly into the phone, turning his back so Chloe wouldn't hear. He'd always called his mother Mommy, but suddenly he wondered if it sounded childish. At first there was silence on the other end. Then he heard his mother draw in a long, shaky breath. "What is it?"

"Where are you, Beta?" his mother asked. "Beta" means "son" in Urdu, and he wished she wouldn't call him that. It sounded as if she'd been crying. "I'm sending Javed for you immediately." Javed was his father's driver.

"Why? What's wrong?" He kept his voice low. His mother was usually calm and reserved. She was not like so many other Pakistani-American mothers: overprotective, disapproving, and subject to panic at the most normal things.

"It's your grandfather," she said. "We're leaving this afternoon for Lahore."

"What's happened?" Jimmy asked.

"He's had a stroke, Beta," she said. "It sounds bad. Daddy wants to see him before . . . as soon as possible. Your grandfather asked for you. He said we must come now, and then he lapsed into a coma. We're taking the three-forty flight. We leave home by one o'clock sharp." That was less than two hours away.

"Tell Javed to meet me at the corner of Van Ness and Market," Jimmy said. "I'm going there now."

Jimmy folded his cell phone and dropped it back into his pocket. He wondered what a coma felt like. Was it like being asleep and not being able to wake up? Was everything dark? He held out his hand to Chloe, who took it and held on.

"I gotta go," he said, his face coloring. "It's my grandfather." His throat tightened and tears prickled behind his eyelids. Chloe squeezed his hand. "He's . . . It sounds bad."

"Go," Chloe said. "Don't waste time talking to me. Come back soon." She let go of his hand. Jimmy felt as if a giant fist had him by the heart, it thrashed and hammered so hard inside his chest. He turned to look back at her three times as he walked off the pier. She stood there with the sun shining on her head like a halo.

When he got home, his mother was rushing back and forth from the laundry to his room. A leather suitcase lay open on his bed and a metal trunk sat near the door.

"How long are we staying?" Jimmy asked as she brushed past him with an armload of folded shirts. She didn't answer and he followed her back to the laundry. "You don't have to pack *all* of my clothes—school starts in two weeks. . . ."

"Jameel," she said, turning, "I don't know how long I should be packing for. Your grandfather is very ill. Uncle Omar said the doctors don't expect him to recover." She resumed bustling and looking worried.

A few short hours later the three of them were seated in the business-class section of a jetliner bound for Pakistan with 7-Up in plastic cups sitting untouched before them on fold-out trays. Jimmy was in the window seat. Cabin attendants were spreading stiff white linens on their trays and distributing packets of plastic forks and knives.

Jimmy's parents seemed not to want to talk. His father stared straight ahead, and his mother put on her earphones. Jimmy concentrated on his MP3 player, but thoughts of death, darkness, and not being awake ever again kept pushing their way into his mind.

After dinner he reclined his seat and summoned a vision of Chloe on her skateboard, sailing from the ramp like a beautiful bird to the beat of Audioslave, her golden, chin-length hair fanning into a perfect circle around her head like the rings of Saturn. That was the thing about Chloe: she was not afraid of anything. She saw everything in a clear light. Jimmy loved that about her.

He awoke some hours later with the inside of his mouth feeling like paper. His father still stared straight ahead. He hadn't even loosened his tie. His mother was staring at him. "What?" Jimmy mouthed, but she smiled softly and closed her eyes again.

Jimmy pressed his forehead against the window beside him. The stars shimmered against the blue-black sky like diamonds on velvet. Some appeared closer than others, and as he watched other celestial objects floated in and out of his vision. He leaned forward to get a better view. They looked like people wrapped in sheets. One figure floated closer, a hand outstretched. Jimmy recognized Grandfather's twinkling eyes, white beard, and arched black eyebrows. Their eyes locked. Grandfather tilted his head, and sadness fell over his face. A chilly breeze blew through the airplane and Grandfather slipped back, stretching toward Jimmy. Jimmy tried to reach out, but his hand bumped into the window. He watched until the figure disappeared among the stars.

Jimmy turned to his father. "Daddy, Grandfather's gone," he said, shivering. His father drew a blanket around Jimmy's shoulders.

"Why do you say that, Beta?" he asked.

"I saw him. He was . . ." Realizing how ludicrous he sounded, Jimmy stopped.

"You've been dreaming," his father said, and patted his cheek. "Go back to sleep. We'll have a busy day when we get to Lahore."

They arrived just before noon. People looking for familiar faces among the travelers jostled at the metal barricade outside the arrival area. Asrar, Grandfather's secretary, waved and made his way to the end of the barricade. Asrar touched his forehead, bowed, and turned to clear a path through the crowd to the VIP lounge. As the lounge doors closed behind them the din gave way to cool and quiet.

Jimmy tried to imagine what Chloe would make of how his family was received all over Punjab province. Everyone knew them. Grandfather was head of the Amirzai tribe. Uncle Omar was a Provincial Assembly member. Amirzai lands spilled from Punjab into Baluchistan, several hundred thousand hectares in all. Chloe's life was so different—she could never imagine how different, he thought.

Jimmy wondered at first if Chloe lived in the streets of San Francisco because she spent so much time skateboarding at Pier 7. She told him she lived in the Tenderloin, on Turk Street, with her mother. Some of the guys made fun of her because she seemed to do nothing but skateboard. The grip tape on her board was tattered, and the deck had been reglassed many times. But she was the only one who could do a full McTwist, and her eyes were as blue as the Pacific. Jimmy's stomach ached at the thought of her.

Jimmy's uncle Omar was inside the lounge. He embraced Jimmy's father and then Jimmy, and then led them to silk-covered chairs arranged in a corner of the lounge. Asrar ordered tea for them, and left to get their luggage. Omar cleared his throat.

"Father died last night," he said. He covered his mouth with his fingertips, cleared his throat again, and went on. "He never regained consciousness. The end was peaceful." Tears welled along the rims of his eyes. Jimmy's mother lowered her face into her hands. His father and Omar both gave Jimmy a long look but otherwise his father didn't react.

"There is much to do this afternoon," said Omar, and he filled them in on details for the funeral to be held before sunset, and for a dinner afterward. Jimmy's mother protested that a dinner was not appropriate for a Muslim funeral. But Grandfather had insisted. His father and uncle seemed restrained.

Outside Jimmy felt as if his eyelids were made of sandpaper as he squinted against the sunlight. The damp, hot, heavy air seemed to part before his face as he walked. The family stepped into the air-conditioned car. The driver pulled out of the airport and a jumble of cars, motor scooters, trucks, and buses shrieked and rumbled around them. When they reached the Cantonment area, the willows along the canal and houses with broad lawns felt familiar. But comfort did not settle over Jimmy in the home of his ancestors. Pain cut somewhere so deep inside him he couldn't identify exactly the place from which his grandfather had been excised.

They turned into 5 Jinnah Enclave, and a hand settled on Jimmy's shoulder. He turned his head but no hand lay there, though he felt its warmth through his shirt.

The car pulled into the courtyard and stopped before the red sandstone facade of Grandfather's house. Auntie Leyla stood in the shade with his cousins, Muti, who was fifteen, Jimmy's age, and Jaffar, a year younger. They saw each other once a year, but the three of them were close. Muti's eyes looked puffy. She and Jaffar watched awkwardly as he hugged his aunt. Usually they jabbered away, catching up on each others' news.

Servants hauled their suitcases and trunks up the winding staircase in the front hall to the second floor. Muti smiled and nodded slightly so only Jimmy noticed. It was their signal to meet in the back garden. She spread the fingers of one hand down at her side to indicate five minutes. Jimmy had written Muti about Chloe, but the news seemed remote and insignificant in light of Grandfather's death. Muti had loved Grandfather as much as Jimmy had.

Jimmy excused himself and bounded up the stairway. The walls of the front hall were painted with almond blossoms and fruit trees, and melons on vines. The ceiling was ornately painted and studded with bits of mirror that sparkled and reflected light from a huge crystal chandelier that hung from the center of the ceiling.

Upstairs Jimmy gazed around his similarly painted and mirrored room and thought again how blown away Chloe would be. He changed into a light cotton shalwar kameez, relieved to be out of a shirt collar and heavy jeans. He ran down the back stairway, sandals slapping at his heels, out into the big garden to a carved wooden gate that led to a secluded arbor, where he found Muti in a swing near a little fish pond.

Muti was crying, the tears spreading like wet veils over her cheeks. He sat down beside her. She wiped at her face with the end of her dupatta, sniffing loudly. "I'm so glad you're here, Jameel," she said.

"I thought Grandfather would live forever," Jimmy said, realizing as the words came out how true they were. "I can't imagine life without him."

"Things have been so strange here," said Muti. "My parents don't let me out of their sight. And last night after Grandfather died and we'd gone back to bed, something woke me up. I went out into the hall and I swear I saw a light outside his room."

"Maybe your father took a lantern with him to sit with Grandfather," said Jimmy.

"The flame wasn't contained in anything, and nobody was there," she said. "This morning I got up to dress, and my clothes . . ." She stopped. "It sounds crazy . . . they were rearranged in my closet." Jimmy stared at her, but before he could say anything his father called him.

"Jameel! Where are you?" He sounded irritable. Jimmy stepped out into the main part of the garden near the swimming pool. Muti followed. "This is no time to disappear." His father's eyes flickered toward Muti. "And you two shouldn't be out here alone." Jimmy was too surprised to answer. Since when did he and Muti need a chaperone?

His father led him upstairs to join with the other men in the ritual bathing of the body. They worked quickly, with tenderness. Jimmy washed Grandfather's hands, and felt the weight of the old man's immense bones covered with strands of muscle and paper-thin skin. When they were finished they wrapped him in a seamless white shroud, which they tied at both ends. Jimmy thought his beloved Babakalan looked like a sack of mail, and tears burned the back of his throat.

He excused himself and went to his room to change into the silk shalwar kameez and vest laid out on the bed by his mother for the funeral. Someone tapped gently on the door and Jimmy crossed to open it. The Maulvi Inayatullah, Grandfather's spiritual advisor, stood in the doorway.

"May I have a word?" he asked. Jimmy let him in. He thought of the maulvi and Grandfather talking late into many nights, arguing, pounding their fists on the table. Grandfather sent for the maulvi whenever an important decision had to be made. The cleric wore a white shalwar kameez and a white turban. His face was round and smooth, although his figure was thin and bent. His beard was wispy but his eyes were clear and his voice was strong.

"Your grandfather wanted me to speak to you," said the maulvi.

"I feel him here with me," said Jimmy. "I've felt his hand on my shoulder. I've seen him. . . ." He paused, not wanting the maulvi to think he was silly. But the old man nodded, and Jimmy told him about seeing his grandfather through the airplane window.

"How like him to be a light in the darkness!" the old man

JAMEEL AND THE HOUSE OF DJINN {39}

said. "He is with me, too, whispering in my ear, telling me my business." He smiled briefly.

"Muti has seen things too," Jimmy said. He told the maulvi about his cousin's clothes rearranging themselves and the light in the hallway.

"Ji," the maulvi said, nodding. "I also have seen disembodied lights."

"Are they Grandfather, too?" asked Jimmy. "What's going on?"

"The thing about lights," said the maulvi, "is that they're brightest in the darkest darkness. The hand on your shoulder may have been your grandfather's spirit, unwilling to depart until he's certain things are settled here. I believe these strange lights are djinn, and they are a different matter. The Quran says God created a djinni for each person. Everyone has one—like a mischievous companion. The djinni's job is to lead you astray, to cause mischief, possibly even to harm you."

"What are they?" Jimmy asked. His grandmother used to frighten them with stories about djinn when they were children. Jimmy had never believed in them.

"They're fiery beings that can fly and take the shape of animals or humans—or any shape, really. They can pass through walls."

"If Allah is merciful," Jimmy asked, "why would he purposely create something to harm us?" In Grandmother's stories the djinni always played dirty tricks. In one of her favorites a djinni stole a piece of jewelry and put it in the pocket of a trusted servant.

"Allah created us with free will," the maulvi said, scratching under his wispy beard. "He made djinn to lead us astray so we struggle to find our own path. We value truth the most when it comes through difficult experience."

"So in the end djinn are good?" Jimmy asked. The maulvi nodded.

"Perhaps they take the form of light because they lead us to knowledge," said the maulvi. "That has a kind of djinni logic."

Jimmy already knew what his path would be: he'd finish school, go to Stanford University, study physics, and perhaps invent things. He didn't need his own djinni.

"But I didn't come to talk about djinn," the maulvi said. "Your grandfather wanted you to take his place as leader of the Amirzai people." Jimmy stared. The old maulvi must be wrong. Uncle Omar was Grandfather's eldest son. He should lead. Jimmy's father would be next in line. "He asked me to tell you, and your father agreed I should."

"But I don't even want to live in Pakistan!" said Jimmy, his voice cracking. It would mean giving up his school, his friends, Chloe, his home, his dreams.

"Your grandfather's spirit has lingered to help you find your way," said the maulvi. "Perhaps he's enlisted help from the djinn. Think about it and we'll talk later. It's time to go now."

The family spent the rest of the afternoon in the grand formal parlor, receiving guests who came to pay their respects. Muti sat with the women on one side of the huge main hall. Jimmy sat with the men on the opposite side, his mind racing. Tradition was such a powerful force here—and he knew he had no choice. He gazed at Grandfather's shrouded body. How could his enlightened Babakalan—the person he loved most in the world—force him to give up his life and his dreams?

The governor of Punjab was first to move down the front row of seats where Jimmy, his father, and Omar stood to shake hands. Next came members of the Provincial Assembly, then tribal leaders from all over Pakistan, followed by doctors, lawyers, businessmen, ambassadors, consuls general and other prominent Lahoris. Finally an army of farmers from the Amirzai tribal lands, many of whom had walked through the day in bare feet, formed a line that snaked around the garden, through the front gate, and formed a throng of thousands in the street. Jimmy's father glanced at him from time to time.

The constant light warmth of the invisible hand on his shoulder annoyed Jimmy, and he shrugged it away angrily. How could his grandfather do this to him?

About an hour before sunset a procession led by the Maulvi Inayatullah, followed by Jimmy, his father, Uncle Omar, and the rest of the family accompanied the body to the park near the gate of the Badshahi Mosque, where it would be buried in a place of honor near the tomb of Alama Muhammad Iqbal, Pakistan's national poet and philosopher.

The rest of the funeral was a blur of faces and hands shaking hands, the maulvi's prayers, and the sense that an era had passed. Jimmy could think of nothing but his anger and his grief, mixed together now and tearing at his heart.

At the festive dinner afterward in the garden at Jinnah Enclave, Grandfather had ordered that men and women should be served together from a common table. The women filled their plates, and then, out of habit, stood on one side of the garden under the shamiyana. The men retreated to the other side. Because no curtain separated males from females Jimmy caught Muti's gaze several times. He could tell by her wide-eyed look of alarm that something was wrong. Twice she tilted her head slightly toward the garden.

As guests began to leave, the party moved indoors, and Jimmy watched for an opportunity to escape to the garden. He began to feel the jet lag, and his eyes drooped.

"Go to bed, Beta," his mother said. "Tomorrow is another day." She kissed him on the cheek and Jimmy felt the hand that had been on his shoulder drawing him now in the direction of the garden. For the first time the hand was insistent rather than gentle, and he had to fight against it to move toward the front hall and the stairway so his mother would see him heading up to bed. The pull on his arm caused him to wobble in a diagonal line between the door to the back garden and the stairway. To end the struggle Jimmy halted under the arch in the entry to the front hall.

"Stop pulling at me," he said under his breath to the spirit that commanded the hand. "You'll land me in trouble." He caught a glimpse of movement overhead and heard a sharp screech of metal. He looked up to see the crystal chandelier his grandmother had bought in Vienna tilt crazily to one side. Another screech and the cables holding it parted and the whole thing, which stood as high as a man and weighed about a thousand pounds, crashed to the marble floor, accompanied by a shower of sparks as loose, bare wires danced under the ceiling. The deafening crash was followed by the absurdly delicate tinkling of crystal drops and beads falling down through the structure of the chandelier onto the marble floor, followed by a chaotic chorus of women screaming, men shouting, and feet running.

Jimmy realized with a shudder that he'd have been under the chandelier if it hadn't been for the hand on his shoulder. The touch was gone now, and in the confusion he slipped out into the garden. There, in the hidden arbor, he found Muti sitting on the swing. Lantern light glinted on the little pond. Small rings spooled outward on the surface of the water, where iridescent koi fed on mosquitoes. Muti jumped to her feet.

"Did you see—" he began, but she was already nodding her head vigorously.

"I felt someone's hand in the small of my back, pushing me out the door," she said. "My feet could barely keep up. I heard the crash, but I couldn't turn back."

"Me too," Jimmy said. "Do you think—"

"Listen, Jameel," she said. Her eyes were urgent and her lips quivered. "We don't have much time. We've got to do something—they're planning for us to marry!"

"You and me?" She nodded and her eyes were wide. He and Muti had shared secrets all their lives. They'd cried when Muti's puppy was killed by a cobra. They'd experimented with kissing and with cigarettes. She was his best friend. But marry her? "Who told you?"

"I stopped by my mother's room to get my white dupatta. She was mending it. She and Father were talking. They stopped when I came in, as if I'd caught them at something. I came to my room to dress. Sound travels through the water pipe. If I move my overstuffed chair out of the corner I can hear everything they say just below me."

"Did you know that I'm to lead the Amirzai people?" She

shook her head. It all fit together now. They would have no choice, unless they ran away somewhere—and surely they'd be caught if they ran.

"There's something else," Muti said, and hesitated. "I have to tell you about someone." She stopped. "It's someone important to me—like Chloe is to you."

"And you haven't told me?" Jimmy felt an odd flash of anger—he felt stung, as if he'd been betrayed.

"Well," she said, "he's totally unsuitable. He couldn't be more wrong."

"He can't be more unsuitable than Chloe!" said Jimmy.

"He's a Hindu," said Muti. Jimmy's eyes widened.

"Where'd you meet a Hindu boy?" he asked.

"He's a tennis pro at the Lahore Club. His mother is Hindu. He grew up partly here, with his father, who is Muslim, and partly in India, with his mother's people."

"Do they know?" Jimmy asked, inclining his head toward the house.

"You're joking! Father's heart would break," said Muti. "Mother would kill me. We meet at the club and sometimes at Choti's. Jameel, we have to get out of here!"

"Where would we go?" he asked. He immediately thought of Choti, who had been Muti's friend since they started school together. Choti's parents were progressive—at least as progressive as Grandfather had been.

"I'm sure we can go to Choti's," she said, flipping open her mobile phone. Jimmy and his parents trusted each other. Why hadn't they told him? The exhaustion that had nearly paralyzed him earlier was gone. He could feel the blood rushing through his veins.

Jimmy looked across the large formal garden behind the house. There was no escape, really. He'd heard stories of young people who tried to run away from arranged marriages being hunted down and forced to marry someone of their parents' choice. One or both might even be killed. He shuddered. His family wouldn't do that, but his father and uncle wouldn't rest until he and Muti were found. He and Muti had no money. And Jimmy's passport was in the safe in his parents' bedroom.

"I can't even get a signal on my phone!" said Muti. "There's a strange howling sound—that's never happened before!"

"The djinn!" said Jimmy, and Muti stared at him. From across the garden Jimmy heard his father calling his name. In the lights around the swimming pool they could see Uncle Omar, Jimmy's father, and the Maulvi Inayatullah making their way toward the arbor.

Servants were sweeping broken glass from the hallway when they came inside the house, which Jimmy realized with a start would soon be his and Muti's house. His mother and aunt were waiting in the parlor.

"We were worried sick when we couldn't find you," said his mother, a frown bunching her eyebrows. "What were you thinking?" Jimmy and Muti exchanged glances.

"We don't want to marry," said Jimmy. "I don't want to lead the Amirzai tribe."

"It's your duty, your responsibility," said his father. "You and Muti have always been close. You're well suited to each other. You don't realize how lucky you are."

"I don't know how lucky I am," said Jimmy hotly, "to never see my friends again, never finish school, or have a life of my own, to be responsible for hundreds of thousands of tribes-men when I don't even know exactly how to be responsible for myself!"

"I'd like to speak to Jameel," said the maulvi. As his family filed out of the parlor Muti hesitated in the doorway and looked back at Jimmy. Then Auntie Leyla took her by the wrist and pulled her into the other room. Jimmy's father stayed behind.

"I know you think we imams are old-fashioned and back-ward, but please listen," said the maulvi. The old man spoke softly but urgently. "You have only one family. If you turn your back on your people you will cut yourself off from them. It will be as if you have no family at all. You can never replace them. That is a serious matter."

The maulvi paused, as if waiting for a response. Jimmy said nothing, and he went on. "The second thing is that 'muhabbat' here is very different from 'love' in America. Our word has to do with tradition, piety, duty, and family. When we talk of ro-mance and passion, immediately we think of sadness or even tragedy. 'Muhabbat' is a serious word. Have you noticed there are few divorces here in Pakistan?"

"I don't care about cultural differences," said Jimmy. "I want my life back."

"Maybe it was wrong that we didn't tell you before," said his father. His eyes were stark in his pale face. "Your grandfather has always wanted you to succeed him, since before you were born. It's his choice, and once made it can't be any other way." Jimmy felt rage boiling in his blood.

"Why didn't you tell me? Why did you let me think I'd be like everyone else? That I'd grow up and make decisions for myself like other people do?" He felt as if he was caught in a time warp—as if he was stuck in medieval times.

"Your grandfather wanted you to graduate from university. He was always healthy, and he thought he'd live to be very old. We wanted you to live like a normal boy for as long as possible."

"When will this marriage take place?" Jimmy asked.

"It must be very soon. Trouble can start if there is a long break in leadership. After three days of mourning, you and Muti will marry."

In the days that followed wedding preparations began. Jimmy thought of Chloe. He wanted to call her, at least to tell her what was about to happen. But he knew it would be incomprehensible to her. He did not see Muti. She was in purdah, in keeping with tradition, secluded before her marriage. Jimmy wondered whether she felt as trapped as he felt.

Jimmy's father made him sit in the front parlor with Uncle Omar each afternoon to receive tribesmen, to hear complaints and solve problems concerning land, crops, or family issues, as Grandfather had done his whole life. Jimmy listened as a tribesman presented a petition to get back a piece of land his cousin had seized. Uncle Omar signed a paper ordering the cousin to tear down the fences he'd built and give back the land. Jimmy wondered how his uncle knew the best thing to do.

Three days passed as if he'd dreamed them. He wished he could talk to Muti and assure her that—what? That he'd be a good husband? That they'd continue to be friends after they married? Gradually resignation took the place of anger. There was no way out. In Pakistan men could be killed for trying to escape their duty.

The third night he went to sleep thinking it was the last night he'd sleep alone. Tomorrow, he thought, and every night until he died he would share a bed with Muti, his wife. It didn't seem real. In the middle of the night he awoke to see a flame hovering over his bed. It was so bright he could not see beyond it.

"Who's there?" he asked. His heart hammered, and he blinked to be sure his eyes were open. The light sped around the room, as if in search of something. "What do you want?" he asked. The light stood still when he spoke. He wasn't scared. He wished Muti was there, and wondered what she'd say to make the djinni go away.

Jimmy reached across the bed for his nightlight and switched it on. The floating light disappeared. He remembered what the maulvi said about light shining in the darkest darkness. He got out of bed and on the table below where the light had hovered was a faded color photograph of a man and woman sitting side by side. Jimmy examined it under the lampshade. It looked like a photograph of him and Muti. He turned it over, and the date, August 27, 1955, was stamped on the back. "Jameel's wedding" was scrawled in faded ink under the date. He looked at the photo again. It was his grandparents' wedding. The date was fifty years ago tomorrow, when his grandfather was fifteen, exactly Jimmy's age.

Jimmy got back into bed and switched off the light. He lay uncovered on the warm sheets, staring into the darkness. In his grandfather's day cousins married to keep property in the family. But the maulvi was right. The American ideal of romantic love had become a part of him and he didn't know how to rearrange his thinking. He thought of Chloe and her golden hair and Pacific blue eyes.

"You and Muti are a good match," said a voice beside the head of Jimmy's bed. He turned to see Grandfather sitting beside the table. A faint white light and a sweetish whiff of betel nut emanated from him. Jimmy raised himself to his elbows. "I felt the same way you're feeling before I married your grandmother," Grandfather went on. "I had a girl in England. And yet your grandmother and I were very happy until her death."

"Babakalan," Jimmy said, "I had so many things planned—"

"And you needn't give them all up," said Grandfather. "Your uncle Omar can handle things here while you and Muti are at university. The experience of living in America will be good for Muti. It will be good for the two of you to live there together."

"But Grandfather, in America—"

"You are not an American, Jameel," he said. "You may have a U.S. passport, but you have the blood of centuries of Amirzai leadership in your veins. You belong here."

"What do I have to offer?" Jameel asked miserably, and his grandfather laughed.

"Just what we need right now is what you offer," said his grandfather. "You honor Islam and you can help make Pakistan a more modern country. You and Muti are strong and clever. You are ancient souls with modern eyes." Grandfather's form began to fade.

"Wait!" said Jameel. "I want you to tell me—about the djinn. And I want to know what it's like where you are. Wait!"

There was no answer as his grandfather's form faded to an almost invisible outline. "Please, Grandfather," he said, "I haven't even said good-bye!" But the figure disappeared completely. Jameel stared into the darkness, and he knew that the djinni had done its job. His grandfather was right. This was his place, and he knew now what to tell Muti.

DHARMA

{ CHARLES DE LINT }

Dharma is fascinated by beatnik culture—its lifestyle, its literature, and, especially, its music. When he meets a beautiful hippie and immediately falls in love, he can't understand why none of his friends see her the way he does. Charles de Lint leaves it to the reader to sort the real from the illusion.

The Summer of Love hit Newford in '67, the same as it did pretty much every big city in North America. Kids flocked to the downtown core—which was kind of funny, since sometimes collecting in the urban center was just the first step in their moving to some rural commune. I doubt they saw the irony in that. For the longest time, neither did I.

I was a city boy, myself. I was born in Beirut, but we'd emigrated when I was five, before the bombing started, so I had only dim memories of my homeland. None of them matched the bombed-out streets that appeared from time to time on

TV news broadcasts. So far as I was concerned, I was a North American, but my shock of black hair and the dark cast of my skin lumped me in with the blacks and Puerto Ricans and all the limitations that being part of a minority entails.

The Summer of Love changed that—at least it did on the surface. And certainly for me.

I lived an unhappy life in an old rundown tenement and was mesmerized by reports of the whole hippie phenomenon. The Eastern mysticism and the drugs. The long hair and the free love. And the music, oh, the music. I'd never heard music like this before. Music that was actually about something more than just boy meets girl, or girl loses boy.

Growing up, I'd already decided I wanted to be a beatnik. A Bohemian poet, I thought. Or a musician. Maybe an artist. I'd dress in black turtlenecks and smoke Gitanes. I'd listen to cool jazz in clubs, getting up to read devastating truths from my notebook, leaning against the microphone, cigarette dangling from my hand. That is, if I wasn't playing in the band—piano, maybe. Or long cool notes on a trumpet.

Where did a Muslim boy get ideas like that?

Not at home, that's for sure. Not at school, either. And for sure, not at mosque.

It took an old guy living down the block to wake them up in me. His name was Mr. Henderson—"call me Ed," he'd always tell us kids, so I did, even though in my head he was always going to be Mr. Henderson. He was probably a kid freak, because his big thing was letting us hang around his house, but he never hit on me or anybody else that I know of. Or at least, no one told me he had.

I liked going there because it was my one escape from the stifling atmosphere at home. He was a bit of a beatnik himself. Played some piano, painted, had written a couple of books. It always smelled like pipe tobacco and old books in his apartment. There'd be music playing—Miles Davis, maybe, or Clifford Brown. He was partial to trumpet players. And he turned me on to all this writing that made what we studied in English class sound like the stuffy old tired crap that it was.

There were poems like Ginsberg's "Howl," which didn't make much sense to me, but I loved the way the words just ran along forever, colliding against each other like confused messengers arriving someplace all at the same time, and not quite sure what it was they were supposed to be delivering. These poems weren't dead words on paper. They were angry and vibrant, confusing and full of life, and I couldn't get enough of them. I read all that I could, which was mostly these little City Lights booklets that Mr. Henderson had. But other books, too. Ginsberg, naturally. Lawrence Felinghetti. Gary Snyder. Ed Sanders.

And of course, the granddaddy of them all: Jack Kerouac.

I took my street name Dharma from one of his books. It meant "the essential nature of the universe or one's own character" and played into my pretense of being East Indian and full of Eastern mysticism and wisdom. I was all about the now, so long as the now didn't include answering to my real name Namir Habib and going to mosque and all the strictures that my old name held.

Mr. Henderson told me how the beat poets were characterized by their angst and anger, but that wasn't what they were really about. They were really all about being alive and living in the moment, and that was all I wanted. Tune in, turn on, and drop out. Although I didn't really embrace the turning-on part. I didn't like the idea of getting drunk or high—not after the first time I tried either.

Drink was a mickey of cheap gin in Fitzhenry Park, after which I was violently sick.

High was some hashish, also in Fitzhenry, and it also made me sick, but in a different way. All I got from it was nausea, dizziness, and the feeling that all my limbs were made of rubber. The guy I smoked it with said that it had been cut with THP or speed—normally it was the coolest, really, he assured me—but I opted to forgo any future experimentation with it.

And anyway, I discovered that I could get high without booze or drugs through meditation and just *being* in the moment. I couldn't make it happen whenever I wanted, the way you can just pop a pill, but when I did connect, it was the best. And it fit in with the persona I'd created for myself.

It was a funny thing, me pretending to be this East Indian swami kind of a guy and nobody calling me on it. I'd run away from home at the beginning of the summer and took up residence in one of the Digger houses—the one off Lee Street, with the big gables and vegetable plot in back—helping out with the collection of day-old food donations we got from bakeries and the like, then doling it out at free suppers the Diggers provided for street kids.

The rest of the time I hung out where all the hippies did. By the War Memorial in Fitzhenry Park. On the Pier, by the ferry dock. Along Williamson Street. I wore raggedy bell bottom jeans with a long muslin shirt that hung to my knees. Beads around my neck, my hair long, my feet bare, the soles filthy from the sidewalk grime. I used to carry around this cotton-and-silk shoulder bag that was all patches of different colors with little bits of mirror decorations—to ward off bad spirits, I'd tell anyone who asked—and in it I kept a recorder and my poetry notebook, a spare shirt, cloths to sit on, and some finger cymbals that I'd pass out when I was playing.

I didn't actually know any real melodies except for stuff I remembered from growing up like "Yiallah Them Rima" and other lullabies. But it didn't seem to matter to anyone that I was only improvising music that I thought sounded East Indian. I'd just play away and people would dance, finger cymbals tinkling. Sometimes we'd be joined by tabla or bongo players.

It was a great scene and I loved it, especially after escaping the strict household in which I was brought up. And instead of getting picked on like used to happen at school, people on the street liked me. I was cool.

When I wasn't working with the Diggers or playing music, my shoulder bag laid out on the pavement for people to drop coins in, I'd have these long involved metaphysical conversations with other people on the street, talking about *everything*. Important things. Poetry and the Vietnam War. The essence of the world and why we existed.

By the time the summer was easing into the middle days of August, no one from my old life would ever have recognized me, and that was exactly the way I wanted it.

I don't know how it got started, but someone came up with the idea of organizing a Be-in for the last weekend of August and before you knew it, everybody was totally into it. Psychedelic posters went up all over town. The Diggers promised food for everyone. There was going to be music and dancing and body painting and everybody just *being*. Being real. Showing the world what our peace, love, and flowers really meant. We were going to be a big middle finger raised up to the corporate and straight world just by the fact that we existed.

I set up outside the gates by the War Memorial early in the morning, my shoulder bag lying open on the pavement to collect coins as I started playing. A tabla player joined me, then a couple of weekend hippie girls—down from the suburbs in their flower-print dresses, their long straight hair falling into their faces as they danced barefoot on the pavement around us.

Other dancers joined us, then some more musicians. Two of them played hand drums, but one of the fellows had an honest-to-god sitar, and what's more, he knew how to play it. He smiled at me, like he knew I was faking it, but I guess in the spirit of the day, he played with me, when he could have played circles around me.

After a while, we had quite a crowd listening and dancing. I gave up all pretense of busking and just let myself fall into the music as people kept streaming into the park to where a stage had been erected and the first of many bands was setting up. Our little impromtu jam broke up when the Lee Street Groovers started their set.

"Those were some interesting melody lines," the sitar player said to me before he left. "Have you ever studied dhrupad or ragas?"

I shook my head. "I'm self-taught. I just play what I feel."

He smiled and nodded. "Well, I like the way you were feeling today."

He moved off into the crowd and I put away my recorder and the finger cymbals. As I was folding the large square of patterned cotton that I used to sit on when I played, I realized that one of the dancers hadn't left with everyone else. She was the smallest girl—I doubt she was even five feet tall—her hair a tumble of brown curls, her gray-blue eyes sparkling with humor and mischief. Just like I'd known that the first two girls were weekend hippies, I knew this one was a part of the real scene, living in a squat or sleeping on somebody's couch. I'd never seen her before, but with the crowds here today, there were a lot of people I hadn't seen before.

She was wearing a tie-dyed cotton shirt that was long enough to serve her as a dress. Around her neck was a beaded choker and a half dozen necklaces dangled down the front of her shirt. Right over her heart she wore a small round tin badge with the word "button" on it that made me smile. I flashed on someone going around putting the names of things on what they were: a little sign on a door reading "door," shoes with the word "shoe" written on each toe.

Lifting the hem of her skirt, she sat on her haunches and grinned at me.

"That was fun," she said.

"Yeah, it was. You're a great dancer."

I'd really enjoyed watching her weave her way in and out of the other dancers, willowy and graceful and always following the mood of the music.

"Really?"

"Definitely. What's your name?"

"Everybody calls me Button," she said, pointing to the badge on her chest.

I laughed. "Which came first? The name or the button?"

"Neither. Or at least, it's not because of this button. I just like to give people buttons. Do you want one?"

"Sure."

She rummaged around in the small embroidered bag she had hanging from her shoulder without looking to see what she was doing and pulled one out. She looked at it and smiled.

"This is perfect," she said as she showed it to me.

It said "unbutton" on it and I found myself hoping that when she said it was perfect it was because she'd like to be with me when things got unbuttoned.

"Let me put it on," she said.

I held myself still as she leaned close and fastened the tin badge to my shirt. Her hair smelled like jasmine incense.

"There," she said, rocking back on her heels. "Now I'm Button and you're not. What's your name?"

"Unbutton?" I tried.

"No, your name name. What do people call you? Do they say, 'Hey, Mr. Recorder man?' Or maybe, 'Hey, Cute Guy'?"

She thought I was cute? I thought I'd died and gone to heaven.

"Dharma," I told her. "People call me Dharma."

"So can I hang with you for a while?"

"You can hang with me as long as you like, but I'm going to be kind of working."

"Bummer."

"It's not like you think. I'm going to help out where the Diggers are putting on their feed."

"Oh, I can do that," she said, and bounced to her feet. "I was afraid you were doing some moneymaking work because today's not the day for that."

I was glad that I'd stopped trying to collect a few coins with my music before she'd started dancing.

In the park, the Lee Street Groovers were well into one of the long jamming blues tunes that they were known for. When I stood up, Button took my hand and did a little pirouette. Then she gave me a tug and led me into the park.

They kept us busy at the Diggers' table, cutting vegetables and bread, serving up brown rice and vegetable curry. But we had each other's company, everybody around us was in a great mood, and then there was the music coming from the stage. We weren't close enough to actually see the band, but we could hear them just fine. The air was redolent with the smells of the curry, not to mention the marjiuana smoke that seemed to be everywhere. It was so weird to see people just lighting joints like this in public.

There were police around, but none of them seemed to be ready to make trouble for us. Maybe because we were just too many. I don't think I'd ever seen so many people in the park—not even for the fireworks in July.

We stayed at the Diggers' makeshift kitchen through the

sets by the Lee Street Groovers and another local band called the Peacenik Collective, but when the Seeds hit the stage—coming all the way from the West Coast to be part of our happening—Button and I washed our hands behind the cook tent, then wormed our way through the crowd until we were right in front of the stage.

I wasn't much of a dancer, and I told Button as much, but she wasn't the kind of girl who let clumsiness or embarrassment be any kind of excuse. She tugged on my hands, pulling me this way and that, until I was dancing, whether I wanted to or not. Truth is, in her company, I wanted to anyway.

Have you ever met those people who just have so much presence that they sweep you into their orbit and you find yourself doing things you might never have done before, things you were pretty sure you didn't much like, but there you were doing them all the same, and enjoying them, too? Button was like that. After a few hours in her company, I doubt I could have denied her anything.

At one point I saw my friend Jasper standing underneath the speakers at the side of the stage in his fringed jacket and Indian cotton pants. He just shook his head to see me dancing and grooving to the Seeds, because I'd told him more than once, "There are players and there are dancers, and I'm definitely a player." But he didn't call me on it. He just gave me a grin and a thumbs-up.

The band finished up with a ten-minute jam on "Pushing Too Hard." Button and I collapsed on the grass when it was done, leaning against each other, laughing and happy. We stayed there watching the last act getting set up—Johnny Thunder & the All-Night Mothers. They were a rockabilly band that had gone psychedelic and were always worth seeing, but Button leaned her lips close to my ear.

"Do you have a place to stay tonight?" she asked.

"Yeah, I've been crashing at the Digger house off Lee."

"Can I stay with you tonight?"

You can stay with me the rest of my life, I thought, because I'd totally fallen head over heels with her. But I tried to be cool.

"Sure," I said. "I'd like that."

"Could we maybe go now? I'm feeling kind of weird."

I sat back a little so that I could get a look at her. While she had a strange glow on her face, that didn't mean much since the colored stage lights were washing over all of us sitting so close to the stage. But she was shivering, so I dug my spare shirt out of my bag and draped it over her shoulders. When I started to move my arm away, she reached up and held it in place, burrowing closer against my side.

"I'm so cold," she said.

It was a warm night, but having seen enough people OD on everything from acid to STP, I could guess what her chills and shivering were from. It was weird. I'd never considered that the free spirit she seemed to be had come from being high. I was a little disappointed. And worried, because I'd seen way too many bad trips.

"We need to get you to a hospital," I said.

"No," she said, her voice muffled against my shoulder. "I just . . . I just need to know that someone cares about me. I just need to be held."

"I don't know. . . ."

"Please."

"But if you're ODing, they can help you."

"I didn't do any drugs."

She was shivering more now and I didn't know what to think. But she had no reason to lie to me and I was so enamored with her that I really would have done anything she asked.

"Okay," I said. "But if you start getting worse—"

"I won't get worse—not if you stay close to me."

"I won't leave you alone."

"I know," she said. "You're a good person." She touched the badge she'd pinned to my shirt earlier. "Even if you're not a button."

Her shivering eased off after a while and she moved so that she could look me in the face.

"Let's just go back to your place," she said. "Would that be okay? I think I'd rather just be with you instead of listening to another band."

"Sure."

I stood and gave her a hand up, then we walked away from the stage, her leaning into me, my arm around her shoulders as we made our way through the crowded park. People were talking and singing; some were still dancing although the music had long stopped. When we got out onto the street outside the park, the usual bustle of traffic and city noise seemed almost peaceful.

I had enough money to pay for two bus fares, so we rode the #2 all the way across town to Lee Street. Button got the chills a couple more times, but after the first time, I didn't say anything. I just let her burrow against me and held her tight, stroking her hair.

It was quiet on Lee Street, even quieter on Waterhouse, where the Digger house stood at the end of the block. There was no one there so we had the place to ourselves. I made us some herbal tea and we took it to the room I normally shared with Jasper and one of the other Diggers, a black guy named Unity. We didn't talk much, just sat close beside each other on my mattress, our backs against the wall, sipping our tea.

"I wish I'd known you before," Button said after a while, her voice small and quiet.

"Before what?"

"Before I found out how ugly the world can be."

I wanted to ask her what she meant, but she didn't explain and I got the feeling that this was something I shouldn't ask about. That I should wait until she told me herself. So instead I told her about myself. What it had been like growing up, what my real name was.

"Namir," she repeated. "I like the way it sounds."

I smiled. "I like the way it sounds, too—when you say it."

She laughed softly.

"It's good to be truthful," she said after a moment, "but sometimes the only real truths are the ones we make for ourselves. You can be Dharma, so long as that's who you truly feel you are. That's what's so good about the world right now. We can be anybody we need to be and who's to say it has to be different?"

"I guess."

She started to shiver again, harder than before, and I got worried all over again.

"I'm so cold," she said. "Just hold me . . . hold me."

We lay down and I pulled a blanket over us, trying to will my own warmth to go into her. After a while her shivering eased to an occasional tremble and I guess we both fell asleep. Or at least I did.

I woke up later and we still had the house to ourselves, but Button was sitting up, looking down at me. I could see her smile in the light coming in through the window from the streetlight outside. She pulled her shirt off over her head, then started to unbutton my shirt.

"I'm not cold anymore," she said.

She pressed her lips against mine and I felt the world go swirling around us, big and full of magic and wonder. It was one of those moments that go on forever and then it just got better when she pressed her naked chest against mine.

"Do you love me?" she asked, her voice a tickle in my ear.

I'd only just met her, but I didn't have to even think about it.

"I do," I said. "I really do."

When I woke up in the morning, she was gone. On the other side of the room, Jasper was snoring softly on his mattress. Unity's mattress was empty, but the bedding was all disheveled so I knew he'd been back from the park. He was probably downstairs already, getting breakfast ready. I'd never met anybody who needed less sleep than he did.

I stared at the empty place on the mattress beside me, unwilling to believe that she was gone. Finally, I got up and went looking for her, but there were only sleeping people everywhere and none of them were her. I found Unity and Sunshine sitting on the back steps and after describing Button, asked them if they'd seen her.

"We just got up, man," Unity said.

Sunshine nodded. "Maybe she went for a walk."

"I guess."

I was just wearing my cotton draw-string pants, so I went back upstairs to get a shirt. As I started to put it on, I saw the badge still pinned to it. Unbutton.

Jasper stirred and turned over to look at me.

"What were you on last night?" he asked.

"I wasn't on anything. What makes you think I was?"

"Just the way you were dancing around by yourself in front of the stage last night. Man, you *never* dance."

"I wasn't by myself."

"Okay. So what were you on, 'cause I wouldn't mind a hit of that?"

"No, I was with this girl. Her name was Button."

When I described her to him, he shook his head.

"There were a lot of people there," he said, "so I guess I just missed her. But she wasn't dancing with you during the Seeds' set. I was high, but I wasn't that high. I would have seen her and it would have made a hell of a lot more sense to see you flinging yourself around the way you were."

I started to get a really weird feeling then and went back downstairs. Unity was sitting by himself, sipping his tea. With the sun on it, his bleached-blond Afro stood up around his head like a halo and made his dark skin seem even darker.

"Remember yesterday," I said. "When we were all getting the food ready?"

"Sure. You were a big help, man. You're always a big help, not like some of the others who just take but don't ever put anything back."

"I was with this girl," I said.

"The one you were just talking about?"

"Yeah, Button. You saw her, right?"

Unity gave a slow shake of his head.

"You were by yourself, man," he said. "Talking away like you had your best friend beside you while you were chopping up the veggies. But there was no one else there. I thought, man, is he stoned or what, you know, and that seemed weird, because so far as I know, you don't ever partake of the weed or anything stronger."

"I wasn't stoned. I . . ."

I had to sit down on the steps beside him.

"But maybe I'm stoned now," I finished. "Because I *know* I was with her yesterday afternoon and all last night."

"She just came to you out of nowhere, and now she's gone?"

"Pretty much.

Unity gave a slow nod. "Maybe you were with one of the spirits, man. An occasion like the Be-in, all the people grooving, it opens doors to the big beyond, you know? Could be some lonely spirit slipped through to visit with you."

"A spirit."

"I didn't see any flesh-and-blood girl working at your side."

I put my head in my hands and stared out at the backyard.

"Do you believe in that kind of thing?" I finally asked.

"I can't say yes, can't say no. I have an open mind."

I turned to look at him. "I can't believe it wasn't real. The best day of my life and I just made it up in my head."

"Everything we experience is real, Dharma. You know that. Whether it's in our head or not."

"My name's not even Dharma."

He laughed. "You think I was born Unity? Man, these are the glory days we're living in. We're not chained to anybody else's reality. We get to be whoever we want to be."

"That's what she said."

"Maybe you should listen to her, man."

"Which is pretty much just listening to myself, considering how I made all of this up."

Unity shook his head. "Not if you decide that, for you, the spirits are real. And only you can make that happen, man."

I didn't feel like Dharma the Eastern mystic right then. I just felt like Namir Habib, stupid and geeky as always.

Unity put his hands on my shoulders.

"You've got it in you, man," he said. "We've all got it in us."

"Got what?"

"The possibility of the world being a better place than somebody else might think it is. But you have to make it happen. You have to believe."

I'm working in a secondhand bookstore these days and I'm thinking of going to night school to get my high school diploma. I could just go back to regular school, but I've lived too big a life in the past year and a half. I meet kids my age who are going to school and it's like we have nothing at all in common. Maybe we never did.

I haven't reconciled with my family yet. My dad can't bring himself to forgive me for running off the way I did. The way he sees it, I've insulted the family, the mosque, my whole culture. My mom's not happy about it either, but at least I get to see her. Once or twice a week, she meets me at the store and we go for lunch together. What surprises me the most is that she doesn't argue with me about the life I've chosen. She just accepts that I've become someone they never expected me to be.

But she still calls me Namir.

I never saw Button again. Not in the world as we all know it, at least.

I don't think this is a ghost story. I'm not sure I believe in ghosts.

I don't know who came dancing to my music outside Fitzhenry Park that day of the Be-in. Who stood at my side chopping vegetables and feeding hungry hippies. Who danced to the Seeds and walked back to the Digger's house with me. Who needed to be held to keep away the cold and then made love with me.

A ghost? A spirit? A dream?

Nothing real, because I was the only one who ever saw her.

But the funny thing is I hold the memories like they really happened.

And I still love her.

And you know what's even funnier? It's been a year since that night, but sometimes she still comes to me when I'm asleep. She comes in dreams and we talk for hours. She tells me she's never cold anymore because I love her. She says she's waiting for me, but I don't need to hurry because she's got all the time in the world.

I always wake up smiling the next morning. When I go to

work those mornings I wear the badge Button gave me, pinned to my shirt. Unbutton.

"What's that mean?" Janey asked me the first time. She's an English major at Butler U. and works at the store part-time, usually sharing a morning shift with me.

"Whatever you want it to," I told her.

DRY SPELL

{ MICHAEL O. TUNNELL }

First, Martin's sister Alyce dies in a fire. Then his mother, Beratha, whom the villagers believe is a witch, also dies unexpectedly. After Martin buries Beratha, he is confronted by strange happenings that compel him to avenge his mother's and sister's deaths. But who could have killed them and why?

The day Martin lowered his mother into the earth, the sun shone without interruption from dawn to dusk. It was a bad omen, the village elders said. Never in anyone's memory had an entire day passed without a good soaking.

Beratha's death had been sudden, unexpected, and so Martin was startled to see the elders standing at the fringes of the forest clearing, casting uncertain glances at the glowing disk that scorched their balding pates. How had they been so quick to find out? How had they discovered Beratha's new forest hideaway? And why had they come out in the heat to witness her burial? He could only guess an answer to his last question: it must be the elders' duty to make certain that the witch was, indeed, dead.

To Martin's surprise, the village priest wasn't among the onlookers. Father Vincent had always kept a sharp eye on Beratha, mistrusting her pagan skills. However, Martin had to admit the wizened cleric wasn't the worst of the townspeople. At least, when blight blackened the crops for a second season in a row, Father Vincent had tried to stop a village mob from burning Beratha's cottage.

Martin touched the left side of his face, running his fingers across the angry scars his broiled flesh had left behind. The mob had barred the doors and windows, making escape almost impossible, but the priest's pleas delayed their arson. The few extra moments made the difference between life and death for Beratha and Martin—but not for Alyce. The heat and smoke had charred his little sister's lungs before he could batter down the door and take her from the inferno.

None of the elders offered an arm for the digging, only silent stares as Martin levered great lumps of yellow clay from his mother's grave with a wooden shovel. At last, as the sun settled behind the trees, the hole was deep enough, and he turned to the seven waiting figures and motioned toward the rough casket he'd fashioned. No one moved to assist in easing Martin's burden into the ground.

He really hadn't wanted their help. Still, the refusal infuriated him. "Curse you!" he cried.

The stern faces, suspended like glistening moons against

the dark foliage, sagged in terror. Wild-eyed, the elders stumbled into the trees and disappeared, not waiting to hear the rest of the witch-boy's hex.

"Idiots!" Martin yelled after the retreating forms. Were they really too stupid to realize he had none of his mother's power? That his mother could work enchantments he had no doubt. Before the fire, the villagers weren't above coming to her for a love charm or a healing potion—but only under cover of darkness so no one would see. Martin, however, had never demonstrated the knack for magic. It was Alyce who had the gift and was her mother's apprentice—her special one.

Beratha was never the same once Alyce was gone. First they'd moved into an abandoned cowshed at the edge of the forest, and there the silence and isolation seemed to match her dark mood. She hardly spoke, and when she did, she mostly muttered to herself. She would leave for days at a time with little or no explanation, returning more taciturn than when she left. Nothing Martin said or did could make her smile. He decided that when Alyce died, his mother had died with her.

Then two village infants were stillborn in succession, and the mob began again to seethe. So Beratha took her son deep into the woods, and set up housekeeping in the tumble-down cottage of a long-dead sorcerer.

Martin's pent-up anguish suddenly surfaced as the last of the elders disappeared. Gulping air to suppress his shuddering sobs, he stepped back and fell against the casket. He allowed himself only a few moments of self-pity, then returned to his grisly task.

Though Martin was large and strapping for fifteen, he

struggled to settle his mother's body gently into the waiting earth. He filled the grave, patting the last handfuls of clay into place as darkness invaded the clearing. It was then that he faced the stark reality: he was alone. No brothers or sisters, no father, no aunts or uncles, and, as a village outcast, certainly no friends. He stared through the murk at his mother's rude cottage, crouching like a great, dark animal at the edge of the forest, and quaked at the prospect of living there without her silent company.

Martin's boots were caked with yellow muck, and he pried them off at the cottage door, also stripping away his muck-coated trousers and tunic. Naked, he crept inside. The night air was uncommonly dry and cool, and he shivered as he stood squinting into the solid darkness. Then he pointed himself in the direction of the fireplace, where he hoped to find an ember nestled under the ashes. Molelike, he blindly inched forward, cursing when he stubbed his toe. At last, his extended hands brushed the rock face of the hearth.

But the touch of the stones was unfamiliar—this was his mother's house but *not* his mother's hearth! Stunned, Martin felt his way along a massive rock wall, far too large for Beratha's one-room cottage, until he stumbled into an opening. As he edged inside, his shin collided with a stone ledge, and with a moan, he collapsed onto it.

When the pain lessened, Martin realized that his bare buttocks were being chilled by the smooth surface of a stone bench, an inglenook within the hearth's mouth. Wrestling with wonder and rising fear, he forced himself to continue searching for the fire pit, but as he was about to stand, the bench began radiating gentle heat. As the pleasant warmth caressed his naked skin, a faint, crimson glow illuminated the hearth's cavernous maw.

Martin stood, backing out of the opening as light from the rose-colored stones intensified. He stared at the hearth's enormity, and then turned to look back into the room. Though he recognized the rough table and stools, the shelves filled with his mother's herbs and roots, and his own straw pallet, they were dwarfed by a space far larger than the outside dimensions of the cottage could contain.

Wide-eyed and trembling, his body mottled with gooseflesh, Martin rooted through the chest at the foot of his sleeping pallet to find his only other pair of trousers and an oft-patched tunic. The coarse fabric did little to warm or calm him, and with teeth chattering, he turned back to the hearth.

As Martin approached the fire pit, he discovered an iron grate the size of a wagon bed resting at the bottom of the deep recess. Cradled in its arms was a single log, a thick cylinder of oak.

More curious now than frightened, Martin cast about for kindling and fagots to add to the grate. Finding nothing, he dropped his hand on the length of oak, grimacing at the prospect of going outside. The log under his palm warmed, and then, with sudden ferocity, flames streaked from beneath his hand. With a strangled yelp, Martin jerked away singed fingers as the bark ignited. In moments, the log was wrapped in flames. As the blaze accelerated, the crimson light from the stones faded. Martin pushed himself into the inglenook, unable to fathom how he'd made fire.

The flames shot outward like striking cobras. Multicolored

tongues of fire coiled and slithered about the surface, and the serpentine movements mesmerized Martin. But then he heard someone calling his name, and his chin snapped up, his eyes clearing. "Mother," he said, peering into the room.

"Martin," repeated Beratha. "I am here."

The sound of his name came from within the hearth, and he turned to find the twisting flames had smoothed into a glassy sheet that reflected his mother's face. Martin slipped from the bench and fell to his knees before Beratha's image. He reached forward with a tremulous hand to stroke her cheek, but the heat stopped him.

"Martin, I am here," Beratha said yet again. "My son, listen with care. You never truly understood that I was capable of far more than curing warts and mixing love potions." In a disconcerting manner, her disembodied head rotated, taking in the surrounding room and the interior of the hearth. "All this was set in place long ago—a manner in which to avenge my untimely death, should it occur. We were never really safe after the fire."

"But Mother, I put you in the ground. How is this poss—"

"If you are seeing me in the flames, I have not died a natural death. I have been slain, and you shall avenge me! From beyond my grave, I shall show you the way."

"But Mother—"

When Beratha's words tumbled over his yet again, Martin realized she wasn't really there. What he was hearing and seeing was a message prepared long before her death. He couldn't begin to imagine how she had accomplished this.

"Are you paying heed?" Beratha asked, and Martin nodded, as if the flickering image of his mother could see him. "You sit within the Great Hearth of the Ancients—the vision-maker of things past. I managed, at tremendous personal cost, to arrange its use for you, Martin. We have little time, so here is what you must know.

"A tree's growth rings record the events that unfold in its presence—an archive of the past unlocked only by the Great Hearth. I am speaking to an oak near the cottage, and you are seeing what it has documented. In this manner, you will seek the identity of my assassins. Whether it be one or many, the trees about our cottage will show you who came here to take my life, for I have been given to know that death will overtake me in this place. Thereafter, you shall find and destroy them. I am certain you will not only be avenging me but also your sister. And as a sign, it will not rain until the murderers are dead—and then not for a year thereafter. The earth shall be scorched for my sake."

Martin recoiled at the suggestion that Beratha had been murdered. He was equally repulsed by the suggestion that he kill someone—anyone. But his mother's apparition gave him no time to protest. Without pause, she launched into meticulous instructions for working the Great Hearth.

The scene in the flames widened so that all of Beratha was visible. Then, speaking as much with her hands as her lips, she began detailing methods for eliminating her enemies: the herbs and powders on her shelves that were poisonous, the ways to administer deadly substances, the most discreet manner for killing with sharp objects, the art of burning dwellings so there would be little chance of escape. That his mother had known such terrible things Martin found both bewildering and alarming.

At last, Beratha came to the end of her instruction. "Your mind is sharp, my son," she said. "If your attention did not wander, you now know all that is necessary to the task. Get on with it, Martin! Avenge me! Avenge Alyce!"

Beratha's image faded, and with a mighty roar, the flames engulfed the pit. A moment later, but for the heaping ashes, the grate was empty.

Martin fumbled his way out of the hearth and managed to find his sleeping pallet. He wrapped himself in his old blanket, its familiar, musty smell comforting him. As he lay staring into the cold, empty darkness, his sorrow and loneliness gave way to anger. They had killed his mother. Tomorrow he would exact a payment for his loss.

The next morning, as the forest wilted in the blinding sunlight, Martin attacked a towering birch with his ax. It stood near the cottage door and would have witnessed anyone entering while he was away. The sun burned his neck and great drops of sweat rolled from his brow. The cloying atmosphere fed his rage, and inside his head, his mother's voice goaded him. *If they took me, they will surely come for you next*, she warned. The tree seemed to take the form of a faceless assassin, and Martin cried out, battering the trunk long after it was down.

When he'd finally caught his breath, Martin hewed a three-foot length from the fallen birch and carried it to the Great Hearth. He concentrated on what he desired to see in the flames, and then ignited the log. He retired to the inglenook, and the warmth inside, coupled with his weariness, had a soporific affect. But just as his eyelids fluttered and closed, Martin heard movement within the fire pit. He sat up, instantly alert, and saw the clearing and front of the cottage materialize within the flames. Two hooded figures emerged from the forest and came to a stop next to the birch tree that now lay burning on the grate. Their voices were barely audible above the pounding rain.

"The boy is away on an overnight errand," one of them whispered.

Martin cocked his head. The voice seemed familiar.

"The witch is abroad gathering roots and herbs for her potions. You will have at least an hour."

At that moment, the rain lessened, and both men threw back their hoods. Martin drew in a sharp breath. One of them was a stranger—a dark-eyed fellow with a pox-scarred face. But Father Vincent's firm chin and beaklike nose were unmistakable.

"You'll get the other half of the payment at week's end, Orrin," said Father Vincent. "Or as soon as I'm certain of the outcome."

Orrin's eyes narrowed. "You need not worry," he said, his accent guttural. "I know my work."

Father Vincent nodded, and then started back to the village. Orrin entered the cottage, and Martin wished he could see what was happening inside. In less than an hour, Orrin appeared in the doorway. He tucked a bundle beneath his robe, and stepped into the rain, which had come again with a fury. He stopped by the birch tree and looked back at the cottage, his harsh laughter audible above the downpour. The flames erupted, reducing the log to ashes, but not before Martin saw Orrin's lips form two words: "Die, witch."

He stumbled from the hearth and leaned heavily on his mother's worktable, his breathing shallow and quick. The priest had hired an assassin, and now Martin was obliged to kill him in return. Oh, to have his mother's magic to aid and protect him. Only Orrin's laughter gave him strength to face the task.

The assassin was an outsider—that was clear from the odd way he formed his words. He was a traveler who would be gone after week's end, if not sooner, and so Martin had no time to waste. He pulled a potent tincture of hemlock from the shelf and prepared one of Beratha's deadly tools, a ring with a pinprick used to convey toxins. He reasoned that Orrin had poisoned his mother, though how he'd managed the job was a mystery. Therefore, it was poetic justice that poison should end his life, too.

There was one place Martin knew Orrin could be found— the village's only public house—and so he wrapped himself in a long, cowled cloak that hid his face and stepped from the cottage. In an hour's time, he stood at the door of the Weary Wayfarer.

The lodgers were gathered in the tavern for the evening meal. With the addition of the town's old men and village loafers, who spent their time quaffing ale and swapping stories, the hall was crowded. Martin found a spot in a corner, no one seeming to notice his entrance except the innkeeper, who sent his daughter to see to his needs. With the few coppers his mother had left him, he ordered a tankard of apple ale, taking care to keep his face hidden. While he sipped, his eyes wandered across the room, but before he spotted Orrin's pox-scarred face, loud laughter—a grating laughter he recognized—drew his attention. The assassin chortled again, tossing a handful of playing cards on the table and sweeping coins from the middle of a game of pairs.

"Are you applying spells, witch hunter?" one of his playing companions said in a loud, accusing voice. "Something you picked up from your prey, perhaps? You haven't lost a round."

Orrin flashed a crooked smile. "My prey do not live long enough to share their secrets," he said, words grinding like gravel in his throat. "I find pleasure in dispatching witch-women—with or without pay—not in stealing the secrets of their dark art."

Martin noticed that a knot of bystanders had started gathering around the gaming table and knew his opportunity had come. He joined the throng, edging nearer Orrin, whose neck was temptingly exposed. He waited until the assassin had won again, a cheer bursting from the onlookers.

The ring pierced the skin just above the hairline, and Orrin slapped at what must have seemed the sting of a horsefly. As Martin pulled the door shut on his way out, he heard a chair tip, accompanied by the sound of something soft and heavy hitting the floor.

That night, Martin lay curled on his pallet, missing the rain. The muffled chatter of drops pelting the thatch, then dripping from the eves, would have filled the lonely silence. He fought the lump in his throat and tried to sleep, only to find Orrin's face behind his eyelids. Another lump rose in his throat, but his mother's voice drove it down. *Orrin deserved to die—he mur-*

dered for money, she reasoned, and her logic seemed to help. Still, he'd killed a man, and nothing could change that, not for the rest of his life.

Do not fear, said Beratha, or a voice very much like hers. *Having done it once shall make killing Father Vincent easier to bear.*

He slept fitfully and arose the next morning feeling surly—and frightened. He was not likely to catch Father Vincent unawares, as he had Orrin. He would have to confront the priest, and he trembled at the thought.

Martin spent the day fretting over how to do the job, and convincing himself he could do it. Whenever his resolve weakened, Beratha's voice would seep into his skull, calling him to duty.

In the end, he decided not to face the cleric at all. Beratha had taught him to use fire; he would burn the rectory with the priest asleep in his bed. *It will be a fitting death to avenge Alyce*, he thought, after convincing himself that Father Vincent's efforts to thwart the mob had been no more than pretense.

He spent several days gathering and cutting wood, and under the cover of darkness, secreting the fuel for Father Vincent's funeral pyre in a copse near the rectory. He also hid several casks of oil to speed the blaze, and some wooden kegs filled with a strange black powder. Properly placed, it would shatter the building—or so Beratha had told him. This was some of his mother's magic, he supposed.

By the time Martin was prepared, a week had passed without rain. He felt a grim sense of satisfaction that his stacks of dry timber would be especially quick to the torch. He waited until well past midnight, until the streets were empty, until the rectory had been long dark. He hauled and stacked the fire-wood with silent care, encircling the small dwelling. At each corner Martin broke open a keg of Beratha's powder, and then sopped the wood with oil.

He was much nearer sunrise than sunset when the task was done. He knelt in the dirt, striking with his flint to light an oil-soaked torch. Concentrating, he did not hear or see Father Vincent until a well-aimed kick sent the torch flying from his fingers. But the priest was old; leaping and kicking had left him breathless. Before Father Vincent could recover, Martin threw himself at the holy man, flattening him. Martin drew his dagger, driving his knee into the priest's chest and holding the point at his throat.

"You weren't supposed to wake up," Martin said.

"Never again, from the looks of things," Father Vincent answered hoarsely. He could barely speak for the pressure of Martin's knee. "I didn't have your mother killed, if that's what you believe, but I know what led to her death. Hear me out, and then if you still need my life, take it."

Martin removed his knee, and Father Vincent greedily sucked in the night air. Using the cord from his cloak, he bound the priest's hands. "So speak," he said, "but be quick about it."

"Do you remember the anguished wailing of our mothers?" asked the priest. "Just before you left for the woods?"

Martin was puzzled. What had this to do with his mother? "I remember the stillborn infants, if that's what you're meaning."

"A funeral with every birth," said Father Vincent. "That is, until yesterday. Yesterday, the village had its first successful birthing in a year—Jostel's Mirra delivered an eight-pound baby girl!

"Some would say we deserved such a curse. We were cruel to you and your mother." He extended a tentative hand toward Martin's fire-scarred cheek, but the boy stepped away. "We would have killed all of you, not just Alyce. I have long sorrowed over Alyce."

"You sorrow for my sister and yet hire an assassin to murder my mother." He rose, pointing the blade at Father Vincent's heart. "And now you dare cast blame on my family for the killing of newborns."

"Yes, I hired someone, but for another purpose. I did not have Beratha killed. I did not, so help me God!" the priest cried. "Martin, I fear you did not truly know your mother. Her magic was considerable, and in the past year it grew dark—exceedingly dark."

Martin aimed a boot at Father Vincent's ribs. The priest rolled aside, catching the blow between his shoulder blades. "If this is true, if her heart and her magic darkened, all of you are the cause," he said, his voice shaking.

"Yes, you are right," answered Father Vincent, wheezing heavily against the pain. "But innocent children were dying. If Beratha was the reason, I needed to know. I needed proof, and that's what I sent my man to find. I said nothing of killing. I hadn't an inkling he would poison her—and would not have known but for his shameless boasting."

"He was a witch hunter," said Martin, his tone venomous. "You should have suspected as much."

Kill him! Beratha's voice raged. Martin grabbed the cord binding the priest's wrists and hoisted him to his feet.

"So you know of Orrin," said Father Vincent, as Martin prodded him forward. "And what do you know of his death?" He sighed when the boy didn't answer. "I knew Orrin would recognize the object in which Beratha had infused the curse—and he did. I can show you."

Doubt swept through Martin, drowning out Beratha's cries. "Then show me," he said.

The priest slipped on the oiled wood as they climbed over it to reach the door. Martin steadied the old man and then shoved him inside. "The charm is in that box," said Father Vincent, nodding toward a small wooden chest covered with pearl-inlaid crucifixes. Martin lifted the lid and stared at the primitive shape of a child in swaddling clothes, impaled with several vicious thorns. The thorns were stained with a dark red substance that also spattered the doll's blankets. An unrecognizable, acrid scent rose from the box.

"The smell comes from within the figure," said the priest as he noticed Martin's wrinkled nose. "It comes from an evil concoction that Orrin was quick to identify.

"Orrin also found a place—a hidden grove. It is a place of magic—both evil and good. It is where Beratha would have created what you see before you. I will take you there, if you wish."

Battered by confusion, Martin pressed his temples between his fists. If he let the priest lead him into the forest, his chance to burn the rectory would be gone, his intent revealed to the village. But if he didn't go . . . He looked up at Father Vincent and nodded, ignoring the increased pitch of his mother's wailing.

The sun was high, the heat stifling, by the time they reached their destination. The old man, hands still bound, stopped before a glistening waterfall. A crystal pool, carved in solid rock by the falls, lapped at their feet. The water was cold and clear, and they dropped to their knees and buried their faces in it.

Without a word, Father Vincent stood and staggered up the incline, stopping at the fall's midpoint. He stepped into the curtain of water and disappeared. "Stop!" Martin cried, and he scrambled after him.

Reaching the spot where the old man had vanished, Martin held his breath and stepped into the icy shower. In two paces he'd passed through the water and stood on a slippery ledge. He followed it to a thin slit in the cliff face, and, slithering through, found himself in a tiny hidden valley. Father Vincent was waiting and led him to a circle of tall stones ringed by ash trees. A rough-hewn altar rested in the center.

One of the standing stones was covered with niches that had been carved into its face. Most of the small receptacles held a talisman or charm. Father Vincent pointed to one of the orifices, and Martin's heart turned cold. The niche held an exact replica of the charm that lay in the rectory. At the sight of the second fetish, fear constricted Martin's heart. Had the priest spoken the truth?

"Orrin knew another must exist to complete the enchantment, but he dared not venture into this place too soon after taking the first. It had to do with a protection spell, he said. To be certain the curse is broken, I need them both. Let me have it, Martin."

Martin drew his knife, and Father Vincent flinched as he lashed out to cut the cords that imprisoned the cleric.

"Take it and go," said Martin. "If you've lied to me, I will come again for you."

Father Vincent moved forward to comfort the boy, whose young face suddenly seemed so old, but Martin pushed him away. "Go now!" he cried.

When the priest's robes slipped out of sight behind the rocks, the noise inside his head faded, and hot tears splashed his cheeks. What was he to believe?

Martin reached the cottage as the dying embers of a brilliant sunset cooled into dusk. He carried a length of ash sapling, the thickest his knife could readily sever. He was relieved, and yet filled with trepidation, to find the Great Hearth had not disappeared.

Before he could change his mind, he lit the fire, and the scene he dreaded witnessing began unfolding in the flames. Arms and legs splayed, Beratha stood within the secret grove. A full moon's silver light flickered through scudding clouds, causing the stone monoliths to drape off-and-on shadows across her face. Lying before her on the altar was a bloody mass, and it took Martin a moment to realize it was afterbirth. He'd seen it often enough during lambing season, but this was different. He shuddered with the sudden understanding that it was human. Where had she gotten such a thing?

In horror, he watched through slitted eyes as his mother—a woman he didn't know, a woman altered by grief and hatred—transferred crimson-streaked bits of tissue to each of the doll fetishes. Her chanting carried evil sounds—phrases in a tongue foreign to him—as she added withered traces of mandrake, hemlock, nightshade, and other herbs and roots he didn't recognize. And finally, Beratha slashed her fingertip and mixed in her own blood. Her chanting became a high-pitched keening that cut off as quickly as if someone had crushed her windpipe.

Beratha collapsed to the rocky soil and lay unmoving. At last, she raised her head, an unearthly gleam in her eyes, and whispered:

"My lifeblood seals this charm of death.
No village babe shall draw one breath."

Martin fled from the inglenook. He threw himself on his pallet and wept. He wept for Orrin. He wept for his mother. For Alyce and the village infants. And he wept for himself.

At last he fell into an unsettled sleep and awoke before dawn knowing what he must do. He wasn't surprised that his mother's smoky fireplace had been substituted for the Great Hearth. It was as if the hearth knew his intent and had fled.

Martin gathered what little he owned and stuffed it into a bag. He rifled through Beratha's things and found another crock filled with oil and two more kegs of the black powder. He dismantled his mother's bed frame and stacked it—along with the table, the stools, the shelves, and the other meager furnishings—in the middle of the room. Dowsing the lot with oil and setting the kegs of powder on top, he stood for a moment gazing at his life. Then he set the burning stub of his last candle on the oil-soaked straw of his pallet.

Martin didn't look back, though the roar of an explosion caused the trees to quake. *I will never look back*, he thought. Then, after a moment, he said aloud, "Well, perhaps someday." With that, a little of his guilt and despair seemed to fall away, and his step lightened as thunder, like sweet music, rumbled through the forest.

Martin raised the hood of his cloak against the rain.

ALLEGRO

{ RICH WALLACE }

Craig's two interests are track and Jessica. "Allegro" follows Craig's visions about how he hopes these interests will develop. The story is told in a crisp and rapid tempo that matches the brisk pace of the race. There are plenty of hints of a possible connection between Craig and a horse Jessica once owned. What do you think the author is suggesting?

Ten hurdles.

You burst out of the starting block and it's step-step-step-*glide* over that first barrier.

Step-step-step-*glide*.

Left-right-left-*glide*.

With me it's more like step-step-step-*bonk*. But I'm learning.

"It's all about timing, Craig," Coach keeps telling me. "Don't jump that hurdle; *drive* right over it. Attack it."

Find a rhythm, he says, like a song in your head that matches the steps of the hurdling.

Step-step-step-*bonk*.

I'm a freshman; I've only been at this for two weeks.

I glance over at Jessica, lean and willowy. She does not glance back. She kneels at the starting line, mouth tight, eyes fixed forward on the ten meters of hard-rubber track between her and the first hurdle. She spits out a burst of breath, enough to rustle a tuft of wheat brown hair hanging toward her eyes. She kicks back one firm leg, sets her fingers on the track behind the line. Settles herself into the starting block. Waits for Coach's whistle.

Jessica is intense. She's aloof. But Jessica knows how to *glide*.

Tuesday morning I take the long way around toward Spanish class and just happen to pass her going in the other direction.

"Hey, Jess," I say, casually but with enthusiasm.

She saw me coming but she acts surprised, looking back as she passes, pretending she doesn't recognize me at first. "Oh," she says, squinting a little. "Hi." She stops walking—a good sign.

"Going to track practice today?" I ask.

"Duh," she says. "Why wouldn't I?"

"Cool," I say. "Me, too."

"Uh-huh."

"We'll probably work on that first hurdle again," I say.

"I imagine," she says. She looks up the hallway, acting bored. "I gotta go."

"Yeah. Me, too. Spanish . . . You got algebra?"

She looks at me sort of suspiciously, like *how would I know that?* I have ways.

"Yes," she says. She starts walking.

"See you at the track."

She keeps going.

Jessica is three inches taller than I am. And she's not quite the warmest person I've ever met.

As she walks away something flutters to the floor and I walk over to pick it up. "You dropped this," I say, but she's gone.

It's a thick coil of what looks like hair from a horse's mane—coarse and a deep reddish brown. It's waxy and almost weightless, shaped into a small circle like a ring.

I read in the *Sturbridge Observer* that the students of the Andante Music School will be giving a First-Day-of-Spring Recital on Thursday evening at Grace Episcopal Church. Jessica is listed among the eight performers. I checked my social calendar and was relieved to see that I am free on Thursday. Also Friday, Saturday, Sunday, and well into next winter.

The freshmen sprinters and hurdlers are running intervals today. Race two hundred meters, then jog the other half lap and race it again. Ten times. I am ready to puke after six, but I go a little slower for the next two and then forge ahead, and the urge to purge goes away.

On the tenth interval I reach deep and outsprint everybody on the final straightaway. Then I clasp my hands behind my head and walk, eyes closed, legs a little wobbly.

"Track!" somebody yells from behind. I hustle over to an

outside lane to avoid getting trampled by some varsity guys sprinting past.

I recover quickly and jog along the backstretch toward my sweatshirt. I'd thrown it on a little pile of leftover snow by the side of the track after the seventh interval, but now the sun's starting to dip and I need it. I see Jessica walking alone through the gate on the other side of the track, heading toward the locker rooms, which are up the path beyond the baseball field and across the parking lot by the gym.

"We done?" I ask the coach.

"Yeah," he says.

"See you tomorrow."

"Wait a minute, Craig," he says.

I've got my eye on Jessica; she's passing the third-base dugout. "What?" I say.

"Think about pacing," he says. "When you start too fast, you've got nothing left for the finish. Sprinting and hurdling, you go all out from the gun, but in a long workout like today you have to pace it out better."

Jessica's reached the parking lot. "Okay," I say. "I get it."

Coach turns and starts yelling at the varsity distance runners racing past. I take off toward the locker rooms at the same pace I ran the intervals.

I reach the gym at the same time she does, but I'm all out of breath. I crash into the door and open it for her, and she gives me a bewildered look. "In a bit of a hurry?" she says.

"Just doing some more work," I say.

She raises her eyebrows and smirks at me, or maybe to herself. She walks up the stairs and reaches for the door to the girls' locker room. " 'Bye," she says.

"What instrument do you play?" I ask, as if we're in the middle of a conversation.

"Violin," she says. And the door closes shut.

I go into the boys' locker room and strip off my sweaty clothes, my running shoes, my socks, and the ring Jessica dropped the other day, which I've been wearing around my right pinky toe for luck.

Thursday after dinner I head toward Main Street. It's rainy and windy and nobody's out. The first day of spring in northeastern Pennsylvania isn't exactly Floridian.

I go into the Turkey Hill convenience store and stare at the magazine headlines:

"Awesome Abs in Fourteen Days."

"Bigfoot Stole My Husband."

"Haunting Music Coming from Elvis's Grave!"

I buy a package of Yodels and go outside. I walk close to the buildings to avoid the rain, and cross over Main Street by the Rite-Aid drugstore. I head down Eighth until I reach Church Street, then walk along the old slate sidewalk toward the Episcopal church.

There's a small crowd of people milling around in the back of the all-purpose room, and the musicians are warming up on the stage. The audience is mostly adults, the men in jackets and ties. I'm in grungy denim pants and sneakers, but I take a seat in the first row of folding chairs and wait for the concert. Jessica sees me and rolls her eyes. Am I being that obvious?

They begin. I have no idea what any of the songs are, but I listen and watch and it isn't so bad. Jessica is wearing a long tan dress that shows her curves, and her hair is pulled back and wrapped tight. Her lipstick matches her dress. She does one short violin solo and one longish one, and the audience gives her rousing amounts of applause. She is obviously good—confident and in control. The same way she runs the hurdles.

A guy a little older than us with curly black hair and sideburns also does a violin solo, but mostly they all play together at once.

Many of the people in the audience are holding pamphlets that I assume tell you what songs are being played. It's all classical stuff that I wouldn't know the names of anyway, but it sounds sort of tangy and pulsating, and some of it gives me a chill.

I duck out at intermission, but I enjoyed it.

Today I am a thoroughbred, racing full speed, my mane waving in the breeze and my flanks shining with sweat as my hooves land gently and rocket off the track.

Step-step-step-*glide*.

Step-step-stutter-stutter-*bonk*.

I take a few more strides and ease up, turn, and jog back to the start.

"Better, Craig," Coach says. "You had it. Trick is to get right back into that rhythm after the hurdle. Drive through it and go."

Yeah. I make two fists and shake 'em a little, bouncing up and down on my toes. It's coming together. I finally ran that first one right—quick start, good acceleration, nice smooth blast over the hurdle. Just string ten of those together and you've got yourself a race.

Warm day—the first one this year. First time it's been mild enough for shorts and a T-shirt. Everybody seems faster. Varsity guys are whipping around the turn on their intervals; the sprinters are charging out of the blocks with more pop. First meet is a week away. You can feel the energy.

I get down in the blocks in lane three and take a deep breath. There are five of us freshmen hurdlers on the boys' team; the other four all hurdled in junior high. I played baseball, but I couldn't resist track any longer. I've always been fast, but hurdling takes lots more than speed. Skill, control, focus.

"Take your marks," Coach says, and I settle into the block. "Set." I raise up my butt and get ready to spring. "Go!"

Drive forward. Stay low. Step-step-step-*glide*. Step-step-step-*glide*.

All right! I glance around as we slow to a walk. I was a half step ahead of everybody. Not bad. The ring on my toe is working.

"Okay," Coach says. "Nice job, boys. I want six two-hundreds, then jog a mile and hit the showers. Tomorrow we'll run some full flights of hurdles."

Good deal.

Funny how when you've got your mind on something else, the thing you've been hoping for happens.

It was the one day in weeks when I wasn't looking for her on my way to Spanish class, hurrying along because I was late and basically just thinking about *speed*. And there she was, blocking my path in tight faded jeans.

"Hi, Craig," she said. She looked sort of defiant.

I caught my breath. "Hey," I said.

"How'd you like the concert the other night?" she asked.

"Great," I said. "You were terrific."

"You left halfway through."

"Yeah. I had homework." I do all my homework in study hall; I left because it was too intense for me.

"You missed the best part."

"That's a shame."

Her hair was down. At track practice it's tied up, in school it hangs down. The concert look was something altogether different.

"You must practice a lot," I said.

She shrugged. "About an hour a day. I'm not *that* committed. Some nights it's only five minutes. Sometimes I'll go for five hours."

I glanced around. The hallway was basically empty now, and in another thirty seconds we'd be late for our classes. Think I cared?

"How do you find the time?" I asked.

"You just do."

"I guess."

"When you love something it isn't a chore, you know?"

"Yeah," I said. "Like sports for me."

"I suppose," she said, "yeah. Trouble is, I don't love it like I used to."

"No?"

"No. Or maybe I do. I don't know. Maybe I just need a break."

I looked up at her eyes. Greenish. I stood a little taller but still felt like a shrimp. She shifted her hips and I caught myself staring. She looked kind of boyish; am I allowed to think that? You know, tough, like maybe she couldn't kick your butt, but she'd be willing to give it a try. And after that, you wouldn't mind making out with her. Wouldn't mind it at all.

She could tell I was checking her out, and she gave what might have been the first flicker of a smile she'd ever given me. "Better get to class," she said.

"Yeah." We started walking in opposite directions. I stopped. "You love hurdling?" I said.

"Sort of," she said, taking a step back toward me. "What I enjoy about it is a lot like what attracted me to the violin. Being in control of yourself, making yourself a tiny bit better every time you work at it. I like that it only really matters to me, when you come down to it. I want to excel for myself. What about you?"

"Yeah, I like it," I said. "More than I expected. I came out for track because I wanted to sprint. You know—pure animalism. I balked at it when Coach told me to try hurdling, but I'm liking the intricacy."

"Big word."

"Big brain."

"I'm sure." She shrugged again, nodded her head up the hallway. "Algebra," she said.

"*Español.*"

"See you at practice."

"And I'll see *you.*"

"What's that supposed to mean?" she asked.

"What?"

" 'I'll see *you*'?"

"Just that I'm watching."

She squinched up her face a little and made a *pfff* sound with her lips. "Concentrate on the hurdles."

"You make it too hard to."

She rolled her eyes and shook her head, but she still had that hint of a smile. "Grow up, chump," she told me.

Step-step-step-*bonk*.

Is this a dream? It doesn't feel like a dream. I am a young horse romping in the stable, so full of energy and excitement. Do they not see that I am a horse at a gallop, free of pressure, free of rules, simply free to run as fast and as furiously as I desire? I feel it in my heart, in my four limber legs, in the entire horseness of my existence. I am not human today.

Today is important. Time trials. Freshmen don't get to race very often. We've got three actual all-freshman meets scheduled (duals against Carbondale and Western Wayne, plus a relay meet over at North Pocono). Our only other chance to race is to be good enough to run varsity. If I can be in the top six on the team I'll usually get to run in the slower heat of the varsity meets.

Coach keeps reminding me to get a song in my head, but I haven't hit on one yet. Jessica probably knows one.

The six upperclass hurdlers race first, and there's a decent-sized gap at the finish line between the first three and the next. I think I can slip in there, make the varsity right off the bat.

I take off my right shoe and remove Jessica's ring from my toe. I want to make my own luck today.

Coach calls us five freshmen to the line and we strip off our sweats and step up. The guy on my right has significant body odor. He's mumbling under his breath, angry or nervous or both.

"Take your marks!"

At the gun I explode out of the blocks and make a clean get-away. First hurdle, no problem. Second one, too. I nick the third and come down off balance, but recover in a hurry and clear the fourth. I'm in the lead now and feeling great, thinking about crossing the finish line, and that tiny lack of focus costs me. Fifth hurdle I slam with the bottom of my foot, but it topples over so I don't lose all my rhythm. I hit the sixth one harder but stay on my feet, stumbling forward and cursing. I have to jump almost straight up to clear the seventh hurdle, and my trail leg hits it hard. And I'm down, catching myself with my hands, my knee skidding on the track. I scramble up and hit number eight, hit number nine, hit number ten and stumble across the finish line in third place.

I shut my eyes and mouth an obscenity. It's like dominos—once you knock one over you can't stop yourself from hitting the rest. That was terrible.

"Good one!" Coach tells me.

"You kidding?"

"No. Nice aggression. You keep at it. Catch your breath and try it again."

I nod. My knee is bleeding, but it's superficial. Coach has other freshmen and the managers adjusting the hurdles for the girls' race. Just one heat—Jessica's the only freshman girl so she's racing with the varsity. She's focused on the track, standing in front of her starting block and surveying the hurdles. Five hours playing the violin? I can't even stay focused for the eighteen seconds it takes to run a race.

They charge out of the blocks and Jessica is right with the leaders, efficiently clearing one hurdle after another. Step-step-step-*glide*. Left-right-left-*glide*. She finishes a close second. Impressive.

I reach into my warm-up jacket and take out the ring, which I should have been wearing but wasn't. I slip it onto my toe and redo my shoelaces. Then I run another flight and manage to stay on my feet, clipping half of the hurdles but not really whacking any. I finish first this time. Who knows what that'll be worth.

"What I love is basketball," Jessica tells me, sitting on the track behind the starting area and pulling on her sweatpants. "My parents made me quit after seventh grade. Too risky." She holds up one hand and wiggles her fingers. "They got all paranoid when I sprained this one fielding a line drive in softball. I couldn't practice the violin for a couple of weeks, but I survived. It was far more traumatic for them than for me."

"So no more contact sports, huh?"

"That's what *they* think. I still play pickup hoops whenever I can. And I'm going out next year for sure. I play at the Y against people on the varsity and I hold my own, no problem. I mean, I'm five-eleven and I know how to play. I love the violin, but I'm not exactly headed for Carnegie Hall."

"Is that what your parents want?"

"Of course they do. They think I'm so terrific because I'm their daughter. But I've been to music camps with some of these prodigies. I'm not in that league. No way."

"You're a heck of a good hurdler."

"Yeah. I could be." She stands and stretches her arms above her head, looking over at the high-jump pit. "You could be, too. I've been watching."

She's been watching me? I guess I'm hard to avoid, since we're in the same event, but has she been watching for other reasons, too? "Do you hear music when you're hurdling?" I ask. "I mean, is there some song with the same pattern as your footsteps that helps you keep your rhythm?"

She laughs. "Never thought about it," she says. "I hear something. Not exactly a song." She zips up her sweat jacket. "That's interesting. My violin instructor tells me I need to sing more—I can't sing worth a darn—but so I'll be better at hearing the music as I read it. Not just seeing instructions for finger movements, but to be better at transforming a symbol on the page into a mental sound. A sound in my head."

"Mmm-hmm," I say.

"Could you tell at the performance the other night how bored I am when I play?" she asks.

"No. You . . . no, I couldn't tell."

"Well, I guess I'm okay when I'm performing. But I'm bored stiff with practicing. Most nights I just sit in my room and play along with rock and jazz CDs, just improvising. My parents hate that. They think you have to be so stoic and solitary to be a violinist."

"Don't you?"

"Yeah. Maybe. Maybe I'm not cut out for it."

"Maybe," I say.

"That guy?" she says. "The other soloist?"

"The one with black hair?"

"Yeah. James. He's always taking on this stuff that's way

over his head—Mendelssohn, or *Tchaikovsky* even. I mean, who is he kidding?"

"Yeah." Like I know what she's talking about, right?

"I mean, he can't even do a three-octave scale with any consistency! So arrogant."

"Yeah. I hear you."

She shakes her head. "He's so competitive."

"I've never seen him before," I say. "Who is he?"

"He goes to Scranton Prep. He's a junior. I know him from the music school . . . obviously. Anyway, I don't know why I brought that up. I mean, I love to compete in sports, not music. Two very different things. At least they should be."

"Yeah," I say.

"Did you hear what he played the other night? A *Viotti!* And everybody sat there like it was so darn *marvelous*. I mean, it wasn't exactly flawless, you know?" She bends and picks up her spikes, then shakes her head and frowns. "Boy, that guy pisses me off sometimes. Viotti! Give me a break."

When I need to think, I do it best if I'm in motion. Not sprinting, and especially not going over hurdles, but climbing hills or jogging in the cemetery or galloping out on the back roads.

Saturday afternoon I need thinking time. Jessica was nice to me at practice again this morning, making little jokes about my hair (tufts of it are always sticking out to the sides) and saying "Good run," after I smoked everybody in a four hundred-meter race at the end. Could she not see how I had been transformed into a four-legged creature, how the running was now second nature to me, so much a part of who I am. How the warm breath flowed so freely from my flared nostrils as I raced, my legs pumping two by two, my tail erect and the spirit of my body so obvious and powerful and equine.

Coach told me I'd be running in the second heat of the hurdles in Monday's meet, as part of the lower echelon of the varsity. I feel that I can win. I feel that I can whinny.

So I head for the cemetery about four o'clock and just walk circuits around the perimeter, up and down the wooded hills, over the rutted back paths. I've never asked a girl out before. Never said, "Hey, you want to go to the movies?" or "How about we get together some night and eat pizza or something?"

So I'm walking my third loop around the cemetery—each loop takes about twenty minutes—and I'm feeling a little less agitated because I've been practicing lines like that and they sound as if they might work, and it's getting dark and I'm coming up that steepest grade over by the stand of hemlocks, just reaching the peak of it, and as I start down I see a big black shape about thirty yards ahead of me, down in the thicket where the paths intersect. It's a bear, lean from the winter but sizable, biting into an old deer carcass that he must have dragged out of a gully. He's got blood on his muzzle and is yanking on the stringy meat with his teeth.

I stop abruptly and just watch the bear for a minute, then slowly back up a bit and walk down the other side of the hill.

I hurry home and put on some music, lively stuff because I'm feeling wired and confident. I could even call her tonight; why delay it any longer? Heck, it's Saturday! I take out the ring and run it through my thumb and fingers. It's brought me good luck when I had run with it.

I hesitate by the phone, figure I should do this in person.

Wait until I can see her face, make a judgment about her interest before bursting out with an invitation.

That'll be better. I'll wait until Monday. Right after our first meet. We should both be feeling good about then.

I stared out the windows during most of my classes today, wishing the day would get the heck over and the meet would begin. And then around sixth period I started hoping for a rainstorm, hard enough to cancel the meet and give me another day to get ready for this in my head. The race and the thing with Jessica. But the sun kept shining and the hour got closer, and now I find myself in front of my gym locker, swallowing hard a few times and staring at my spikes.

I've got time. There are a couple of relays and the sixteen hundred meters before we race, so I walk to the starting area to stretch and try to relax. *You want to go to the movies? You want to go eat pizza?*

Jessica is lying flat on the track over by the fence, stretching out her arms, then bringing her knees to her chest. She glances my way and gives a little smile, so I get up and walk over. I'm thinking about what movies are playing, what she'd like to see, but I can't come up with anything.

"How you doing?" I say, standing over her, looking down.

"Nervous. You?"

"Some. Just want to get going. I'll be fine once I get in the starting blocks."

"Yeah. I didn't sleep worth a darn last night," she says. "Whenever I nodded off I'd be in a race, and the hurdles kept moving farther away every time I approached them."

I laugh slightly. "They only move when we hit them."

"No kidding. I finally got up around one-thirty and played for two hours. Took my mind off racing. Got me in a rhythm."

"That's good. You want to—" I stop myself.

"Want to what?"

"Um . . . jog? Loosen up a little?"

"I already did," she says. "I just need to stretch awhile. You can go ahead." I reach into my warm-up top and pull out the ring. "You dropped this," I say. She looks surprised. "Just now? I've been looking for it for days."

"A few days ago. I forgot I had it."

She smiles broadly and kisses the ring. "This is my good-luck charm," she says. "These are hairs from my horse's mane. I made them into a ring."

"Hope it works for you today," I say.

"Me, too." She looks at the ring for a long moment. "He died three years ago. Too young . . . His mane was the same color as your hair."

I hear the gun and see the relay runners taking off. I figure I've got fifteen minutes. I take a deep breath. Worry about her later. I've got a race to run.

I jog off, away from the track and out the gate, where I can be alone. *Maybe we should hang out sometime. Celebrate our first track meet. Eat pizza at the movies. Want to?*

Coach issued our uniforms on Saturday, and I wore the jersey under my clothes during school today. Nice smooth material; feels good against the skin.

I get back to the gate and I see Jessica over by the bleachers, leaning against the fence and talking to someone. It's that guy

James, the violinist. They're talking about something in a friendly way. She touches his arm. Then she laughs.

This looks bad.

I block it out. I get down into a sprinter's start and wait for the imaginary starter's gun, bursting forward for a few strides. I ease to a stop, bounce up and down, then walk back.

They're still over by the fence. She pushes her hair back behind her ear and leans toward him. The guy looks like a real jerk. He's a *junior*. Find somebody your own age.

Forget this. I don't need the distraction. I sit on the track and reach for my toes, just feeling the nice stretch in my hamstrings, thinking only about the race. Drive over those hurdles, attack them.

She finally makes her way down the slope and over toward the starting area. About time. The hurdles are next. I take a deep breath and stand up. The guys in the first heat are adjusting the starting blocks and stripping off their sweats. I put on my spikes and double knot them.

"Good luck, Craig," she says.

I exhale. Check my laces again.

"I said, good luck," she says.

"Thanks."

"And good luck to me, too, *huh*?" she says. I catch the edge in her voice.

"Yeah," I say, a little sharper. "Good luck to you, too."

"What's your problem?"

"Why is *he* here?" I say.

"Why shouldn't he be?"

"I thought you didn't like that guy."

She flicks up her eyebrows. Gives me a half smile. "No," she says, drawing out the word, teasing a little.

No, she *does* like him, or no, I'm wrong?

I look at her. She rolls her shoulders forward, then back, loosening up.

"I thought he was your competition," I say.

She lets out a little laugh. "No," she says. "I'm thinking maybe he's yours."

I stare at the back of the hurdler in my lane, locked into the starting position, waiting for the gun. It fires, and the six runners blast out of the blocks. I shut my eyes. I'm up next.

She grabs my arm. "Come on," she says. "Kick some butt."

I breathe out hard. Leap straight up a couple of times.

"So," I say. "At least I'm in the race, huh?"

"Yeah," she says. "You're in it."

Clear your head, I'm thinking. *One hurdle at a time.*

I adjust the blocks, stare up at that first hurdle in my lane.

Luck.

My first major test. Intricate. Animalistic.

You can't win the race if you don't enter.

DEPRESSING ACRES

{ PATRICE KINDL }

From the first day she meets her new neighbor, Mona is convinced that Mrs. Duck is dangerously evil. Children in the neighborhood are disappearing, and the parents don't remember that they ever had any children. Mona worries that Mrs. Duck's next victim will be her four-year-old sister, Joy. She fights desperately to keep Joy away from Mrs. Duck's grasp, but no one will believe Mona's frantic warnings....

"My, what a pretty little girl! Wouldn't you like this nice candy apple?"

A wrinkled, bent old woman stood on the front porch of the house next to ours, holding out a neon red apple. The moving van had left half an hour ago and my little sister, Joy, and I were watching from our yard, hoping to see who had moved in.

"Maybe not, Joy," I whispered, thinking of poisoned candy and razor blades.

Joy pretended not to hear me and started across the lawn.

"Hello," she said, staring with open wonder up into the lady's face. There are no old people in our neighborhood, and I guess she'd never seen anybody that ancient before.

"Ah, the darling! What a lovely, lovely little creature you are," crooned our new neighbor. "Here, my sweet, this is all for you." Joy is four, and she *is* pretty cute.

Joy's sharp white teeth crunched down on the candy apple.

"And what are your names, now? I am Mrs. Duck." Her voice had a foreign lilt.

"Missus Duck!" Joy cried gleefully, through a mouthful of gooey apple.

"Shut up, Joy," I said. "That's Joy, and I'm Mona. We live next door to you."

Mrs. Duck didn't seem able to take her eyes off my sister. "Joy! A lovely name for a lovely child. Do you like kitties, Joy?"

"Kitties!" agreed Joy with enthusiasm, wiping her sticky palms on her pants.

Mrs. Duck clapped her hands sharply, and cried, "Droop! Drool! Come!"

Immediately two slithery gray shadows poured themselves over the edge of the porch and landed at Joy's feet. She uttered a cry of delight and crouched over the two cats.

"Nice kitties!" She picked them up the way little kids do, clasping the head and forequarters to her chest and leaving the body to dangle. They hung there passively, regarding the world through disillusioned eyes.

"Droop 'n' Drool!" she squealed. The cats flinched and their eyes closed.

"Joy," I said. "Put the kitties down. You'll hurt them."

Mrs. Duck cawed with mirth. "That dear creature couldn't hurt them if she tried. You must come see me sometime, Joy. You and I and the kitties could have a lovely time."

Joy smiled at her. Young as she was, she knew that this was always a good move.

"Oh, what a *darling*!" breathed Mrs. Duck. Her nostrils flared as though she had just smelled something delicious. "You're sweet enough to *eat*!"

A fingerling of cold air slid down my spine.

"Put those cats down." To Mrs. Duck I added, "We have to go. Good-bye."

Joy lavished another smile on Mrs. Duck and suffered herself to be dragged away.

"Well, I must say, I think it's very kind of her. She only moved here two weeks ago and she's already watched the Enderley's baby and those Collins kids, too. For free!"

"Watch it, Mona. She'll be cutting into your territory."

I lifted my head from the book I was reading. I hadn't really been listening.

"Huh?"

"That nice Mrs. Duck next door wants to take care of Joy while we're out at your recital Saturday night," said my mother, nibbling at a square of chocolate. "This fudge is absolutely delicious. Try some, you two."

"What?" I sat up.

"Don't worry, Mona," my father said, helping himself to a chunk of fudge. "There's more than enough babysitting business in Depressing Acres to go around."

We lived in a development called Refreshing Acres. My parents call it Depressing Acres because all the houses are almost exactly alike. They're little and plain and, well, cheap. We can't afford anything better yet. We were going to move into a nicer house but then Joy got born and that took care of that for a while.

It's the kind of neighborhood where young couples buy their first "starter" houses. There are no other teenagers around, just babies and toddlers. So my babysitting services are in high demand.

There's no landscaping in Refreshing Acres, and it's really flat, so you can stand on a cross street and see through fifteen identical backyards. This is kind of weird on summer Saturday nights when everybody barbecues—every yard has a father, a gas grill, a plastic swing set, and a kiddy pool, all in a line stretching from Apple to Yew Street.

"*I'll* watch Joy," I said now, thinking about Mrs. Duck.

My parents looked at me in surprise and then laughed.

"How? Do you have second sight?" My father licked chocolate from his fingers.

"You'll be onstage, remember? And," Mom added, forestalling my next suggestion, "it'll go on too late for Joy to come. I'll be surprised if we make it home by midnight."

I sat silent for a few moments, trying to figure out how to explain my objection.

"Have you seen Mrs. Duck's lawn lately?" I asked at last.

"Since she lives next door, the answer to your question is yes," said my father.

"Well, don't you think that all those black vines are kind of creepy?"

"She's European—they grow fruits and vegetables as well as grass and flowers. Those are probably blackberries or raspberries. She does a lot of baking, and I suppose she uses the fruit," said my mother. "Don't be so provincial, sweetheart."

"Yeah, but—they're growing *really* fast. Haven't you noticed?"

"Fertilizer," said my mother vaguely, eating another cube of fudge. My mother saw to it that my father and I mowed the grass and that was about it for her and gardening.

The day after Joy and I talked to Mrs. Duck, hundreds of shiny black shoots had begun poking out of the lawn, only a few inches apart. A week later these were vines, studded with razor-sharp barbs. They snaked across the ground, twining about the base of the abandoned slide and swing set, flinging coils around a small sapling.

And now—I stood in the doorway and stared—when had *this* happened? The vines entirely covered the swing set. The little tree was bent in half, close to snapping under the weight. Vines scaled the walls and sealed shut the windows, snarling into an impenetrable barbed-wire jungle.

Standing there with my blood thumping in my ears, I *watched* them grow, stretching out blind, greedy fingers to grasp and climb everything in their path.

A door creaked. It was Mrs. Duck coming out onto her porch. She wore a long black robe and held a braided cord in her hands. One of the cats, Drool or Droop, appeared and rubbed himself on her skirts. She began tying knots in the cord, muttering under her breath and staring out over the neighborhood.

I stilled my breath and stepped back from the door.

In the living room my parents were hunched over the plate of fudge, their mouths and hands smeared dark with chocolate. "Mmm! Try some of this!"

"Mrs. Duck made it," added my mother.

"No thanks," I said.

"It's a curious thing," my mother said at dinner on Friday night. "You know Mae Enderley?" My father nodded. "I was asking after her baby today in the supermarket—I noticed she didn't have him with her and I thought her mother might be here, watching him. She said, 'What baby?' And she just kept going. Isn't that strange?"

"No," my father said.

"Yes," I said.

"She probably *does* have her mother staying with her, and she wants to pretend she's a carefree teenager again," suggested my father.

"Maybe you're right," said my mother.

"Yeah," I said, "but have either of you seen any of the Collins kids around?"

"Oh, they're around," said Mom.

"Bound to be," agreed Dad. "Hey, did the Duck give you any more of that fudge?"

There was a For Sale sign on the Enderleys' front lawn

the next morning and the Collins's house was vacant and echoing.

"Are you ready, sweetheart?"

"I feel feverish," I said. "And my throat hurts."

"Honey, what a shame! Your recital!"

"Guess I can't go," I said. "We'll have to stay home."

"Oh, but—Mrs. Duck is coming and everything. Let me take your temperature."

When her back was turned I held the thermometer to a naked lightbulb. *Beeep!*

"A hundred and five!" My mother gaped at the thermometer. Her hand flew to my forehead. She stared hard at me, then the lightbulb, then back at me.

"Hmmm. Suffering from a little performance anxiety, are we? Don't worry, you'll be brilliant. No, sweetie"—she shook her head as I began to argue—"not another word."

Bing-bong!

Mom went to the door, smiling in an understanding sort of way over her shoulder.

I heard Mrs. Duck's voice from the front porch. "And how fares the fair musician?"

"Oh, she fares fine, Mrs. Duck. Just a little stage fright. Do come in."

"No!" I cried involuntarily. *"Don't invite her in!"*

Mom gave me a pissed-off, behave-yourself-in-front-of-company look.

Mrs. Duck was all in black, with a tall, pointy, wide-brimmed hat. In one hand she carried a broomstick and in the other a chalice trailing wisps of greenish steam. The cats wove figure eights around her as she walked. She cackled at the expression on my face.

"*M-om!*" I pointed an accusing finger at this outrageous vision.

"Pointing is *rude*," Mom whispered. She smiled apologetically at Mrs. Duck and enquiringly at the goblet in her hand.

"It's for Mona." Mrs. Duck advanced on me, holding it out. "A soothing drink."

I backed up so suddenly I hit the wall behind me.

"No!"

"*Mona!*"

"Not a chance," I said.

"Mona!"

"Mom, look at her! Look at the way she's dressed! And will you *please* just go look at her yard? What do you think this is, anyway? Some nice old neighbor lady? I wouldn't drink that stuff if it came with a full chemical analysis and a guarantee from the Food and Drug Administration."

"It's only hot cocoa," said Mrs. Duck placidly.

"*What have you done with the Enderley baby?*" I demanded.

Mom looked like I'd slapped her.

"Go to your room this instant, Mona!"

"Fine!" I said.

"And you're grounded."

"*Fine!* Which means," I said triumphantly, "we won't be needing you, Mrs. Duck."

"Mrs. Duck, I am sorrier than I can say—"

"Weren't the Collins kids enough for you? There were *three* of them!"

"Go! Now! Go, go, go!" My mother rushed at me, waving her arms like I was a flock of badly behaved chickens.

I went. So did Mrs. Duck. She left a box of homemade cookies.

"Have you seen the house next door lately?" My parents both shot surreptitious looks at me. In the days since my recital-that-wasn't, this was a touchy subject. Especially after I made all those phone calls to the Child Abuse Hotline, the FBI and the Department of Health. And of course, after a few of Mrs. Duck's doughnuts, the cops gave me a warning and a federal agent came over and yelled at my parents for about an hour.

"Yes," answered my mother, a little too loudly. "Pretty cute! I understand she's opening up a day-care center."

"The neighborhood needs one," said my father heartily. "See you all tonight!"

I sighed. I put down my cereal bowl and went to the window to look.

The two-bedroom, one-bath ranch house next door was now made of gingerbread. The roof consisted of giant mint wafers, with jumbo-sized gumdrops lining the ridge. The siding and shutters were drawn on with frosting, and there was a six-foot candy cane for a lamppost. The vines had regrouped and reformed into the simulation of a gnarled, prickly forest surrounding the candy house.

There was a whole lineup of cars in the street out front,

dropping off little kids. I saw one kid break off a licorice stick from the mailbox and hand it to his mother. She ate it.

"Wonderful," I muttered. Well, you couldn't say I hadn't tried.

I grabbed hold of Joy. "Don't eat *anything* from the Duck house, you hear?" I said.

My month's grounding was up. I'd barely left the house in the past four weeks, and neither had Joy. But I didn't need to go outside to know how things were. Like I said, you can see a long ways through people's yards around here.

Still, with Joy's hand grasped firmly in mine, I did a tour of the neighborhood.

Every house was vacant. Every house had a For Sale sign out front.

The whole development had been emptied out, except for our house and Mrs. Duck's.

There was no point in talking to my parents about it. I'd tried. They were sort of dimly aware that there were a bunch of vacancies in the district but blamed it on the closing of a local glove factory.

"So," I said, "*everybody* in Refreshing Acres worked there? 'Cause they're all gone."

"Don't exaggerate, Mona."

I shrugged.

The candy house now had morphed into something different. It was bigger, for one thing, and the gingerbread was gray, not brown. No more beat-up family sedans dropped off kids;

instead big, blank-sided trucks began rumbling through our suburban streets to pull up in front of Mrs. Duck's.

Day by day, the house next door swelled like a mushroom in the summer rains. It grew battlements and towers. The briar-forest shrank down as the house ballooned out, to become ivy clinging to stern granite walls that encompassed the entire lot.

"It's a castle," I observed bleakly.

"Yes, doesn't that stone facade look lovely?" asked my mother. "Adds a little class to Depressing Acres. We need it, with so many houses for sale."

"If you say so."

Then I found a vine creeping onto our lawn. That was a shock—I'd assumed it was bound to its own lot, but here it was, nosing its way over the boundary. Of course, in the past people had been obliging enough to bring their kids *to* it. Now the kids were gone.

Except for Joy.

I sent Joy inside. She complained, but I was firm. I grabbed an ax from the garage and aimed a mighty blow at the vine. The ax bounced right off. I whacked and whacked and whacked at the thing, then dropped to my knees, my chest heaving.

It grew an inch.

I needed another weapon. After a quick sweep of the house and garage, I found a butcher's knife, a big pair of pruning shears and a saw. Then I added the fireplace poker to my collection and brought them outside.

I sawed and chopped until my hands were raw. It sprouted leaves.

Infuriated, I lifted the fireplace poker, my last tool, over my head and brought it down as hard as I could.

Sssss! The vine began to steam. Slowly it shriveled and shrank and dwindled. It was gone.

I closed my eyes in relief.

"What exactly do you think you're doing, Mona?"

"Mom!" I held up the poker. "What is this made of?"

"That is a very nice wrought-iron poker that your father bought me, and I'll thank you to give it back to me this instant. I've about had enough of—"

"Okay, what about these? What metal, I mean?" I indicated the other tools.

"What is the matter with you, anyway? Steel, I suppose." She began gathering up all my implements, including the poker. Thoughtfully, I followed her into the house.

"Where's Joy?" I asked, looking around.

"Who?" Mom looked confused for a second. "Oh, the bedroom, I suppose."

I opened the door to our room. She wasn't there. What *was* there, in the open window, was a flower. A huge purple flower on the end of a vine, polluting the air with a sickly sweet smell of peppermint. And, of course, the vine led directly back to a window in the fortress next door.

Mom was watching me from the hallway. "Give me the poker," I said.

"I will not! Mona, you are just acting crazy lately."

"Give me the poker!"

She put the poker behind her back and shook her head.

"Then . . . then . . ." I looked around me wildly, "what else is made of iron? Come on, Mom, quick!"

"Iron?" She backed away from me. "Nothing much is, anymore. Why—?"

"I want," I said through gritted teeth, "something made out of iron."

"Uh . . . um, iron—the ironing board?" she gabbled. "No?" Her eyes fell on a jar of vitamins on the sink in the bathroom. She pointed. "Iron supplements?"

"Are you crazy?" I snatched up the bottle. "*Iron supplements? What am I supposed to do with a vitamin pill?*" I shook it at her, the pills rattling.

"Anything you like, dear." Mom had this weird, frozen smile on her face. I rolled my eyes. Oh well. Presumably they *were* iron. I shoved them into my back pocket.

The flower, I saw, was busily making tracks, retreating toward the castle. Scrambling out the window, I caught up with it before it vanished into the wall. I grabbed the flower by the throat—it squirmed and flailed around like a mad thing—and using the vine from which it grew, I hauled myself up the wall and over the windowsill.

I was inside Mrs. Duck's.

It was an enormous room, filled with children. For some reason they all seemed to have plastic bags on their hair. Some bent over huge vats of simmering liquids, some over conveyer belts. It looked a lot more like a factory than a castle inside. The smell of chocolate, caramel, and mint was so overwhelming I nearly gagged.

On three of the walls were fifteen-foot-high posters of Mrs. Duck smiling and holding out a platter of treats. *Grandma Duck's Old-fashioned Desserts*, they read. *They're So-o-o-o Good for You!*

"Hello, Mona. How nice of you to join us." It was the witch.

I stood up, rubbing a painful knee.

"Where is Joy?" I demanded. "What have you done with her?"

"Your sister? Oh, she's here, somewhere. Joy? Come!"

She was calling my sister just like the cats, I noticed. And, just like the cats, Joy obeyed. One lollipop was tucked inside her cheek, another she held out to me.

"Hi, Mona. Have a loppilop." Joy always called lollipops loppilops.

"No! Spit that out. I *told* you not to eat anything of hers!"

Joy frowned. "I like loppilops. Missus Duck says I can have all the loppilops I want."

"You see?" Mrs. Duck said. She wheezed a phlegmy laugh. "Admit it! You thought I ate them all, didn't you?"

I had, of course, thought exactly that. "I—"

"Oh, no! With minimum wage what it is these days? I needed them on the assembly line. Now, the babies," she added as a second thought, "*those* I ate."

"*What!*"

"They're no use otherwise, the babies aren't," she explained. "Joy, dear, help me take care of your sister—she'll have to be restrained. Give me some of that."

" 'Kay," said Joy, trotting over to a vat of viscous pink fluid.

"*Joy!*" I gaped at my sister.

"Gloves, Joy, gloves!" Mrs. Duck chided. "What did I tell you? Hygiene, please!"

"Oh yeah," Joy said. She donned some clear plastic gloves from a box and scooped up a mozzarella-cheeselike string of goo.

"*Joy!*"

Mrs. Duck took the string and flung it at me.

The world became shocking pink, with an overwhelming odor of artificial strawberries. I found myself struggling against powerful elastic bonds. Finally, I lay exhausted, mummified in fuchsia-colored rubber.

"Bubble gum," said Mrs. Duck. "Now you just chew yourself loose and we'll talk business. I've a job for you. We'll discuss it when you're free." She hacked out a laugh.

"Juh! Juh!" I mumbled, but Joy was gone, following Mrs. Duck.

I nearly bit at the stuff but stopped just in time. No, once in my mouth it'd turn me into a zombie like everybody else. I thumped my bound feet in rage.

The vitamins? Pretty pathetic, but they were all I had. I squirmed and struggled until I got a hand inside my back pocket. Then, hands and bottle had to be manipulated to the front so that I could unscrew the lid and prize out a pill.

I pressed the capsule deep into the bubble gum. And— nothing.

It didn't work. Maybe they weren't iron. Or maybe I was wrong about the properties of iron. Frustrated, I crushed the capsule between my fingers.

Something gave and one of my hands came free. The chewing gum was ripping. *Of course!* The iron was inside the capsule—it couldn't work until it was opened. Quickly, using both hands now, I tore the chewy pink bonds from my body.

Soon I was free. Sticky and flecked with pink, I sat up and looked around.

"Well, that certainly didn't take long! You've got an impressive pair of jaws," said the witch, suddenly appearing in front of me.

The vitamins! I thrust the bottle under my left hip and smiled vacantly.

"I'm busy just now, so the discussion of your duties will have to wait. Just walk around and see to it that everyone is working, will you, dear?"

I nodded and staggered to my feet.

In twenty minutes I had done the entire circuit of the castle/factory, furtively unscrewing iron supplement capsules, dumping their contents into every vat. There still remained the packaged goods, but—

"What are you doing, girl?" Mrs. Duck's cold bony hand closed on my wrist.

"Nothing," I said.

"Let me taste that!"

"Sure," I said, holding out my spoon. . . .

I was always grateful that the Enderleys never came back asking what happened to their baby. The parents of the surviving children showed up, though, offering various reasons for leaving their offspring with Mrs. Duck for so many weeks.

"She was such a *nice* old lady," explained the mothers.

"And a *great* cook," said the fathers.

No one could believe Mrs. Duck would just abandon thirty-nine children and walk off like that. "No one" included the FBI agent, who showed up on my doorstep two days later.

He eyed me in silence, then said, "So, kid, what did you do with the old lady, anyway?"

I nodded to myself. Yes, I had been right to put a little something aside for this exact situation. I smiled.

"Come in," I said. "I think I can explain it all to your satisfaction. But first, I have some fudge I'd like you to try."

RED SKY

{ S. L. ROTTMAN }

The world is on fire. Barely ahead of the spreading inferno, a few are running for their lives. One by one they drop off, until only Kief and Hybream are left. Will they ever reach safety? Rottman's vivid descriptions create an atmosphere of suspense that draws the reader into the story.

Red sky at morning, sailors take warning;
Red sky at night, sailors delight.

What did it mean, I wondered, when the sky was red morning *and* night, *and* all day long?

But that was a stupid question, because I knew exactly what it meant. It meant the world was on fire, and had been for a long time, for too long.

I wasn't sure how long the world had been burning, but I knew that I had been running from the fire for almost a month. And for the last week, I had run alone.

There were five of us who had started together, when the outer edges of Cuskey had begun to light up. Others believed that Cuskey's inner firewall would save them, and they had stayed. The flames had moved with frightening speed, and we had not been out of the city for more than two days before we saw the inner towers topped with flames.

We had to move fast, every day, and the journey took its toll on all of us. McAllae, the oldest at seventeen, had been the first to drop. One day after lunch, he had decided he needed a nap.

"A nap!" Jobans, one of the six-year-old twins, had exclaimed. "You're way too old for a nap!"

McAllae had shrugged. "I need the rest," he declared.

I didn't believe him. He had been the first one up each morning and he was always successful scavenging for food. He couldn't be in better physical shape. He was telling the truth, though—he was tired. Tired of running. Tired of the idea of running.

"Come on, McAllae," Kobans urged. "We don't want to stop yet!"

"You go ahead, squirt. I'll catch up by nightfall."

But he never did.

The six-year-old twins, the youngest of our group, had fallen two days later. They had slowed us down from the very beginning, but after losing McAllae, they seemed unable to keep a steady pace. One morning when we woke up, we could already feel the heat of the fire. But a mere hour after breakfast, they had stopped to rest.

"We can't stop yet," I said, eyeing the red storm behind us.

"We have to," Kobans had said.

And no begging or pleading would get them to move for nearly two hours.

When the sparks began to come through the air, Hybream and I had been able to get them to move again, but not for very long.

It only took us thirty minutes to get ahead of the sparks, but Jobans and Kobans had stopped ten minutes after that.

"We can't stop!" Hybream had wailed. "We have to keep going!"

"So go," Jobans said listlessly. "I need to rest."

"Me too," said Kobans.

So we sat and waited with them again, although every fiber inside me was screaming to run. When the first sparks came flittering down, Hybream and I both stood up. The twins, however, did not.

"We have to go," Hybream said urgently.

"Now," I insisted.

They refused to move.

Hybream and I looked at each other, and without saying a word, I bent down to pick up Jobans while Hybream picked up Kobans.

We didn't make it far.

The twins, although they looked small, were heavy. And Jobans, at least, wasn't even trying to hold on to me. It was awful. We were already running on exhaustion, and every step cost too much.

Hybream started to cry as she set Kobans down. "I can't," she sobbed. "I'm so sorry, but I can't."

Wordlessly I set Jobans next to his twin.

This time I couldn't look at any of them as I started walking. But I hadn't even taken three steps before I could sense Hybream walking next to me. I refused to let myself look back, refused to let myself see one or the other of the twins staring after us.

Hybream never looked back either.

The tears streamed silently down her face nearly all day, but she never looked back. Not even when I thought I heard a scream.

I liked Hybream, even though I hadn't met her until we all decided to run. We were all orphans, and although the few remaining adults at Cuskey had tried to tell us we had to stay, they really didn't have any power to keep us.

We walked fast, quickly putting the drifting sparks behind us. Hybream was up to the task, and before we stopped for a quick dinner drink from the river, we had gotten away from the heat of the flames.

"Maybe it's slowing down again," she whispered.

"Maybe," I said, not believing it for an instant. But for three or four days, we stayed ahead of the heat, even gained a little ground. The sky became more pink than red.

But that didn't last long. Too soon the sky turned red again, and the air blowing off the river didn't seem as cool as it had.

The last night she was with me, the fire had gotten close enough for us to feel the heat blowing towards us again.

"We'll never make it," she had fretted.

Although I wanted to contradict her, I didn't know how without telling an obvious lie.

She had curled up next to me, studying the river. "Do you ever want to just sink underneath the surface and forget everything?"

"No!" I shuddered. I had never learned how to swim, had always feared the creatures that lived beneath the water. I wouldn't even wade in it, and had to force myself to put my hand in long enough to fill my water jug. The only reason I stayed close to the river was because I knew that it promised an unburnt path in front of me.

"I do. I dream about it. About slipping under and dreaming forever."

I shifted slightly so I was between her and the river.

"How old are you, Kief?" she asked suddenly.

"Sixteen." Not quite, but almost.

"I'm only fourteen," she said.

"Just a baby," I teased.

"Kief, have you ever kissed a girl?"

"No," I admitted in a low voice.

She sat up a little and looked at me. This close, her eyes were a startling dark blue, even in the red glow. Then she closed her eyes, and pressed her lips to mine.

It was soft and nice, but seemed more like a kiss I thought I might have gotten from an aunt, if I had one. When she pulled back, those blue eyes were brimming with sadness.

"I'm holding you back," she whispered.

Again, I chose silence over lying to her.

"Without me, you could travel twice as fast."

"Let's sleep," I had suggested, "so we can both travel fast tomorrow."

She had smiled sadly but hadn't argued with me. She got up and spread her blanket out a few feet away from me (and I admit I felt a flash of disappointment).

I slept soundly, as I always did. The others had complained of nightmares and restless nights, even when we were still in Cuskey. After the twins, I was sure I would have nightmares. But my sleep was dark, and solid, almost like one long blink. Usually I woke in the same position I had fallen asleep in.

My nightmares came during the day, plaguing me the whole time my eyes were open.

My eyes snapped open, and I knew something was wrong. That was saying something, since nothing had been right for so long.

Hybream's blanket was still there, wrinkled and wadded up as if she had had a rough sleep. But she wasn't there. And I knew that if I were to go looking for her, I wouldn't find her using the bushes or washing up at the river. She was gone, just like everyone else.

I closed my eyes again, and wished that sleep would take me, wished that I could take a final nap and let the fire sweep over me. But there was something inside that drove me on, that wouldn't let me rest. Something that seemed to be calling me. I had been leading our group, always deciding which way to go, and no one had challenged me. If they had, I would have gone my own way. Maybe they had heard the calling, too.

My eyes were open again and the sky was pink above me. Hybream had been slowing me down, but she had traveled faster than the twins, and we had made good time. Today, though, today I would really move. Maybe by the end of today I would see a grayish sky above me before I closed my eyes.

For four days I had been under a pale not-quite-blue sky that turned completely black at night, and it was a beautiful thing. But now I had nowhere to go. The river fed into a large body of water, of course. And I was pinned in the corner that the river and the ocean? lake? formed.

I hadn't been idle as I waited, hoping the fire would stop for some reason, hoping that maybe it would turn away from where I was. While I'd been hoping, I had constructed a raft from the deadwood along the riverbank. It had only taken me a day and a half to build it, and it was as sound as I could make it.

I hadn't tested it yet.

Instead, I spent the rest of my time gathering food, and looking for water jugs or containers I could use to keep water.

I knew I should leave the shore before the flames reached me.

But I didn't know how long I'd be on the water.

And the creatures of the deep would surely be bigger than what lurked beneath the river.

My sleep was still deep and dreamless. But my nightmare was worse than I thought it ever could be.

The heat was so intense now that I was only wearing my underwear, and I slept on top of my blanket instead of under it. Although the sparks hadn't caught up with me, and I couldn't see the smoke, my eyes stung and no amount of tears cooled them down.

When I woke, gasping in soot and burning smoke, I knew I couldn't put it off any longer. It felt like it was the middle of the night, but the light from the approaching fire made it impossible to judge the time.

I threw my blanket and my pile of clothes on the raft, and checked the stacks of supplies, making sure everything was tied to the raft.

As I pushed the raft out, wading into the water, it wasn't just the smoke and heat that made it difficult to breathe. Fear constricted my chest.

Climbing onto the raft didn't make it any better. The water lapped up through the cracks between the pieces of deadwood, like a beast taking a taste of me. The raft wasn't sturdy enough for me to sit up on, let alone stand, so I had to lie down, which exposed more of me to the water than I thought I could stand. The more the waves kissed me, the more I wondered if death by fire was really such a bad thing.

I could see the flames devouring what remained of my campsite when the end of my raft suddenly rose up. I almost rolled off into the murky depths, but I caught the rope that held most of my food, and it held me, too. After that I lay diagonally, with my head in one corner and my feet in the opposite one, figuring that if one end or the other lifted up again, I wouldn't start to roll off.

Time passed. How much, I don't know. All I know is that I drifted farther from the dangerous safety of the fire-eaten land. The water kept lapping against me. It got so I noticed it more when it stopped.

I ate and drank as little as I could. I slept only fitfully, five minutes here, five there. I couldn't be any more tired, but I was too petrified to sleep.

Eventually, however, my body overrode my mind, and I did sleep. And I woke up just as my raft flipped over, plunging me under.

I barely stopped myself from screaming, from releasing the precious air I had in my lungs. I began to thrash instead, trying to find a way to get my head back above the surface. At first I felt I was sinking farther, but then I got the sensation of lift. Encouraged, I began kicking even harder, my lungs desperate for air.

The top of my head broke the surface of the water, and I opened my mouth to breathe.

Then something grabbed me, and yanked me back under.

Instead of a full breath, I found myself choking on water. I was going down fast, so fast my ears hurt. Whatever had hold of my ankle wasn't releasing me.

Suddenly the water was gone, and I was spitting out water and gasping in air, lying on a slick, hard, cool surface.

"It's okay, Kief," a voice said softly.

I tried to jump up, but only managed to get to my knees. Exhaustion and terror and lack of oxygen had taken their toll; my body didn't want to move anymore. I looked up and stared.

Hybream was standing in front of me.

We were in the middle of a round room. Nothing else was there. No furniture, no windows, no pictures. Just me and Hybream, and a smooth, round, dark blue that melted from ceiling to wall to floor and back again without any lines.

The air felt thick and heavy. After so many days and weeks of heat and dry air, the humidity almost gagged me. I felt water clinging to every pore of my skin.

"Wha?" I sputtered.

She sighed, a deep, happy, content sigh. "I told you I dreamed of sliding under the water's surface. And here we are!"

"I don't—" I broke off. "What's wrong with your eyes?"

"Nothing." She blinked, and her pretty dark blue eyes looked the same as they had before. But for a moment, they had looked—I didn't know how—wrong.

Shaky, I got to my feet. I put a hand out to the side to steady myself, and flinched when I pushed through and my hand was in the water again. I yanked my hand back, and it was dry. I suddenly realized that I was completely dry, even my hair and underwear. "Where are we?"

"In a bubble."

My eyebrows went up. "A bubble? Just a regular bubble?"

She laughed. I couldn't remember the last time I had heard anyone laugh without a hint of fear. Her laugh was full and deep and without worry. "Well, it's a rather *large* bubble," she pointed out.

"And it's staying underwater," I said. Hybream might have thought things were good here, but I couldn't shake the feeling that something was wrong. Bubbles should rise to the surface—especially large ones. "What made this bubble?"

A strange expression crossed Hybream's face, and she said, "You've been through a lot. Why don't you just rest for a little bit? We can talk later."

"I think we should talk now." A large dark shadow moved outside the bubble. "What was that?"

"I really think you should rest."

"Hybream," my voice went up a notch and echoed strangely in the chamber. "What is it? What's going on?"

She sighed and shook her head at me, clearly disappointed. "It's too soon," she said, and I got the feeling she wasn't talking to me. "But if he fights it . . . it doesn't matter . . . he has to know. . . ." She sat down, still muttering and talking to someone else.

Another dark shadow moved, this time below my feet. I tried to see what it really was, but other than the fact that it undulated like a large snake, it was too dark to see any details.

Hhuzzzzaaahhh

A giant whisper filled the bubble, making the hair on the back of my neck stand on end.

"What is it?" I asked again, unable to stop the tremor in my voice.

"They," she said, emphasizing the word, "are the Torches and the Salvation."

"Excuse me?"

"They started the fires, they've kept them going, and they will save the world."

I stared at Hybream, and she just watched me calmly.

"What?"

"I told you it was too early," she said.

"Try again anyway."

"They are older than the dinosaurs. They've survived the Ice Ages and the nuclear blasts and the meteors. They are timeless. They live in the water for centuries, waiting for a time to come to the surface again, to take to the skies and through their fires rebirth the world."

"What are they?" I demanded again. She wasn't telling me anything—but she was telling me everything, if I only listened.

She closed her eyes and when she opened them again, they

were black, inky without any whites or iris showing, just black like a gaping hole.

"They are the past, present, and future. You and I have been selected—us from among so many—selected to ride, to serve, to save."

Hybream shook her head, and I watched in fascination as her hair whipped side to side, faster and faster until it seemed to wrap her in a cocoon, and then suddenly Hybream was gone, and the bubble was gone, and I was thrashing in the water.

Something came up under me, and I found myself straddling a large body, clinging to it as it rocketed to the water's surface.

We erupted from beneath, spraying water all around into the dawn's rosy red. We were instantly airborne, and beneath us all I could see was charred black earth and dark blue water.

I was clinging to a beast covered with scales larger than my shirt. At first I thought it was black, but as it banked a turn, I saw some of the scales reflecting a dark blue. Behind my legs were two powerful wings that stretched and pumped in a regular rhythm, keeping our course smooth and easy. The creature's head was easily twice my size, and trailing behind us was a long whalelike tail.

As we circled the ground, occasionally I could make out the remains of a tall building, automobile, or a swimming pool. Everything had been incinerated. Nothing moved on the ground. In the distance, I saw more large flying shapes, swooping low or spiraling high before gliding down again, occasional bright flames arcing out from them.

Hhuzzzzaaahhh, whirled through my mind again, and we began our descent.

I braced myself, cringing against the thought of diving back into the water. To my surprise, the beast gently landed on the bank of a large lake.

I slid, or rather fell, off and took a few stumbling steps before I could control my shaking knees again.

Quickly I turned to get a better look at the beast that had so graciously carried me, but I was standing alone. I turned in confusion, scanning the sky, but it was empty. I was completely alone.

"Not quite."

Spinning around, I found Hybream standing behind me, a small smile playing on her lips.

"Are you—" I began, then stopped. She was watching me with her dark blue eyes. Was it really Hybream again? "What are they called?"

She shrugged, "Dragon is as good a name for them as any, I suppose. But they're almost more comfortable in the water than they are in the air."

Slowly, I asked, "How . . . how many did . . . did they . . . select . . . to save . . . to ride?"

She tried not to laugh at me as she answered gently, "Enough."

"Now what?" I asked, looking around. "Will they help us? Are we supposed to help them?"

"Yes," Hybream said softly.

It felt like we were the only two on the planet. Nothing moved on the ground or in the water. But as empty as the world seemed, I felt full of possibilities and hope.

"Kief," she began.

"Yes?" I took a step closer to her. She was talking so softly.

She turned her head bashfully, and her hair blew across her face. "Would you kiss me?"

I didn't waste time with an answer. I took the last step between us, and bent down to her face. Just before our lips touched, she opened her eyes.

Her completely blank, depthless, black eyes.

ABRA-CA-DEBORAH

{ DAVID LUBAR }

Deborah knows what to expect when she is the only girl to enter a contest for aspiring young magicians. It's not easy for a girl to be accepted in the boys' world of magic. And when a bratty little contestant tries to sabotage her performance, Deborah must use her own special magic to put the obnoxious boy in his place.

How long before someone says it? Deborah wondered as she carried her equipment through the backstage entrance. She paused to study the crowd hustling around the dimly lit area and decided it would be less than a minute before she heard those hateful words. Bracing for the inevitable, Deborah took a deep breath, enjoying the familiar mingled aromas of shellacked hardwood floors and musty velvet curtains.

Someone spoke before Deborah had a chance to exhale.

"Hey, what's she doing here? She's a girl."

Deborah stared at the speaker. He was a grubby little boy,

maybe five or six years old, dressed in a miniature tuxedo with a too-large top hat on his too-large head. A red clip-on bow tie appeared and disappeared beneath the loose flesh of his wagging jaw like an upside down version of a bobbing apple. His face had been scrubbed and polished, but he still looked grubby. His mother, who was straightening the top hat, made a minor attempt to shush him, but he continued to broadcast his opinions.

"Girls don't do magic. Magic is for boys." The last word came out sounding like "boyzes."

I was right, Deborah said to herself, *less than a minute and they've started.* She'd have guessed the trouble would have started with one of the boys her own age, but it didn't surprise her that a younger boy had spoken first. She felt all the other eyes shift toward her. The boys, as nervous as they must have been, turned away from their cards and doves and rabbits for a moment to glare at this girl who dared to try their craft. She was used to boys acting this way, but Deborah expected better from the mothers. They were women. They should have known how it felt. They should have understood. But they joined their sons and stared at her with the scowl reserved for invaders of sacred turf.

"Girls don't do magic," the boy said again, looking up toward his mother.

The mother gave a small nod.

"This girl does magic," Deborah said, speaking quietly and more to herself than to the angry figures that stared at her. She wove her way to the far wall, knowing most of the eyes still followed her. *I'm glad I didn't wear the dress*, she thought. That would have given them even more to stare at. Deborah knew she looked enchanting in the evening gown. She could be enchanting—that was no problem. But she'd decided to go with a modest blouse and black slacks. When she got on stage, she wanted to be judged on her skills. She didn't want to score points based on any accidents of birth.

As Deborah reached the corner, she could hear drifting bits of whispered exchanges. Bursts of locker-room laughter rose from random spots as boys made their stupid comments. Deborah fought her urge to strike out at them. It would be so easy to let her rage win. For a moment, she savored the thought of lashing back. But that wasn't why she'd come. The North American Magicians' Association was the largest group in the country. If she could win the junior contest, she knew people would have to take her seriously. This was her last chance for the juniors—once she turned thirteen, she'd have to compete with the adults. And as much as she dreamed of winning in the adult division, she knew that it was a whole different world from the juniors.

Deborah blocked out the lingering chatter as she set down her kit. Unlike the boys, she'd come alone. Her mother had flown from the city on business last night, taking another of her many midnight flights.

"Break a leg, kid," she'd said when she'd given Deborah a hug for luck. "But make sure it isn't one of yours."

Deborah didn't mind looking after herself. She wasn't lonely. She had her cat at home, and her books.

As she prepared her equipment, she scanned the room, trying to spot the real competition. There didn't seem to be anyone she couldn't beat. The little kid would be a problem. The judges always favored the youngest contestants, even if they had no real talent. A small kid doing bad tricks from a cheap kit could almost always score better than an experienced young lady performing difficult effects. Other than the little kid, Deborah saw nothing to worry her. Most of the contestants were just hobbyists.

It won't hurt to give them a bit of a scare, Deborah thought. She reached into her kit and took out a deck of cards. The deck disappeared. Then it reappeared. She fanned the deck with one hand, spreading the cards smoothly. The deck, still fanned, disappeared again, only to reappear one card at a time. Not bad, she thought. There weren't many kids around who could back-palm a whole deck. There weren't even that many adults who could perform the sleight this smoothly.

I'm good, Deborah told herself. *I'm very good.*

Still, this one flourish wasn't enough to make her stand out as the very best. Deborah took the effect a step further. She held up another deck in her left hand. Making a special effort to ignore her audience of sons and mothers, she repeated the sequence, but this time she did it with both hands at once. Cards appeared and disappeared with grace and flare. Months of practice, hours each day in front of a mirror, were the only secret here.

"Man, she's good," someone whispered.

"Ssshhh," someone else said. "She's not that good."

Keeping all expression from her face, Deborah put the cards in her pocket and picked up a green sponge ball from her kit. She rolled it across her fingers, savoring the way it waltzed over her hand. She tossed it up in the air. She tossed it again. It changed color. She tossed it a third time. One ball rose into the air—two balls fell. She repeated the sequence with both hands. "Just a girl," she said to no one in particular. *I'm a lot more than just a girl*, she thought, allowing herself a small smile, *but they'll never know the real me.*

Something else grabbed Deborah's attention. She dropped the sponge balls in her kit as the announcer walked in and spoke to the contestants. "Okay, kids, let's get this show going." He read off the order of appearance from a sheet on a clipboard. Deborah was next to last. That was a good sign—in the old days, the top act always went on next to last. Deborah wondered whether any of the boys in the room had ever bothered to study the history of their art. The position also allowed Deborah to see almost all of her competition before she performed. The snotty little kid was the only one who would go on after her.

"I want a soda," he said to his mother.

Speaking of little brats, Deborah thought as she glanced over at him.

"Quiet, Abner," his mother said, "the show is starting."

"*I want a soda!*" he shouted, his mouth getting large enough to eclipse half his face.

"Yes, darling," his mother said, digging frantically in her purse for change. "Mommy will get you a soda." She hurried off.

Deborah shook her head. This kid was a real brat. She turned her back on him and joined the fringes of the crowd as they watched the show from the side of the stage. The first kid wasn't bad, but he was obviously a beginner. He looked nervous, and he didn't know how to use the microphone. He kept talking as he moved around, so his voice would fade in and out. Deborah knew the judges would kill him for that mistake. The next two acts weren't any better, or any worse. Each did a few tricks they'd probably just bought off the shelf at a magic shop, and received polite applause. But Deborah loved magic so much, she didn't even mind watching bad magic. There was something she could learn from any performance. And there was something wonderful about the art. Deborah found great beauty in creating the illusion of magic through skill and cunning. And, despite what these kids said or thought, there had been many successful female magicians. But mostly, women were stuck walking around in ridiculous costumes, wiggling their flesh while handing out swords and taking away doves.

Deborah's dream was to change all that. Nobody was going to saw *her* in half. She wanted to become the world's most famous female magician. *Female nothing*, she reminded herself as she thought about her goal. She wanted to become the world's most famous magician, period. And she wanted to do it through hard work, practice, and skill. *No tricks or shortcuts for me*, she thought as she watched another act. The kid was doing some fancy flourishes with a deck of cards, but it was a trick deck where the cards were threaded together. Deborah knew that any good magician in the audience would immediately spot the gimmick. And the judges were all good magicians. She wasn't going to take the easy way. No gimmicks, no fancy equipment, no special help of any kind.

She watched the next boy. He moved well. Deborah suspected he had a natural talent—but not for magic. He might have made a wonderful dancer, or maybe a mime. He made an adequate magician, but she knew he'd never rise beyond the level of birthday parties and talent shows. Deborah understood quite well that the talent a person was given at birth wasn't always the talent that brought happiness. She had other skills, herself, but magic was where her dream lay.

"You're next," the announcer told her as the boy finished his act with a decent version of the Zombie floating-ball illusion.

This was when the real butterflies always hit. Deborah knew the panic would fade the moment she started to perform. But for now, she had to live with the spasms that rippled through her stomach. She rushed back to the wall and grabbed her kit, then walked onto the stage. As always, the instant she felt the bright lights above her head and the hard wood floor beneath her feet she knew this was where she belonged. She set her kit on top of a stool and reached inside for the silk handkerchief she used for her first effect.

A cold shock stopped her.

Deborah's fingertips dipped into a slimy mess. Bubbles tingled against her skin.

"What? . . ."

For a moment, she stood frozen, not understanding. Then she knew. Realization and anger flooded her at the same time. Someone had poured soda on her equipment. Everything was a sticky disaster. There was nothing she could do. There was no quick way to repair the damage. It was beyond her power. A high-pitched giggle struck at her from the wings. Deborah saw the little beast peering out from the shadows at the side of the stage. He bounced from foot to foot, almost dancing in delight.

Deborah wanted to strike back. But the audience was waiting. She could sense them nearing that moment when a crowd's attention turns from excitement to boredom or—worse yet—to pity. Another instant, and she knew she'd lose them. In the few minutes allowed for each act, there was no way she'd ever win them back if she let them slip away now.

The cards! She had two decks in her pocket. Deborah wiped her hand on her blouse, then reached into her pocket. *Be your best*, she thought. As soon as her fingers felt the familiar surface, she slipped into her rhythm, each hand dancing a slow dance with fifty-two lifelong friends. Within a few seconds, the crowd was caught by her spell—a spell woven from nothing but two hands and two decks of cards.

They were hers. She was magic.

Nothing stood in her way. As she reached her ending, Deborah knew she had stunned them with her skill. Feeling like a figure skater approaching her hardest jump, she pointed to a man in the audience. "Name a card."

"Six of clubs," the man said.

She pointed to a woman. "Another card, please."

"Jack of hearts," the woman said.

Deborah repeated the names, then threw the two decks into the air. As the cards rained down, she thrust her hands into the fluttering cloud. Then she lifted her hands high in triumph, the six of clubs grasped in her right hand, the jack of hearts in her left.

Perfect, she thought. *It was perfect.*

Deborah smiled and bowed. The audience went wild. They clapped and cheered and stomped their feet. The sound embraced her like her mother's hugs. Deborah waited until the applause showed the first signs of dying, then bowed again and turned to leave the stage.

"Girls aren't magicians?" she whispered, smiling even wider.

She said it again as she moved behind the curtain, hurling the words like a missile at one small target.

"Big deal," the boy said as Deborah glided past him. "Watch me." He strutted onto the stage, puffed like a rooster who thinks the henhouse is the entire world.

Deborah knew he couldn't be any good. He had too much hatred inside of him to be a real magician. Magic was born of calm and confidence. But she was still worried. The judges could fall for him because he was little.

He started off well. The crowd liked him, even though he was less skilled than any of the other boys. He made coins appear and disappear. He did it just poorly enough that Deborah was sure the judges thought he was cute.

Deborah studied the judges. They were grinning and nodding at each other. One judge whispered to the man next to him. From where she stood, it looked like he'd said, "Isn't he adorable?"

For a moment, Deborah closed her eyes and squeezed her hands into fists, reminding herself of her vow. She would win through skill and not trickery. She wouldn't win with gimmicks or by draping herself in a slinky dress or using any unfair powers. Deborah wanted an honest victory.

You don't always get what you want, she reminded herself as she watched the little kid. *And life is rarely fair.*

Deborah told herself she should just wait and take her chances. But the boy had played a rotten trick on her. She couldn't help aiming bad thoughts toward him. He was so nasty that some of what he'd done to her would surely have to come back around and bite him.

"Drop them," Deborah whispered. She unclenched her fists and wiggled her fingers.

There was a clatter as the boy dropped a handful of hidden coins. He made a joke about it. The crowd laughed. He started his next trick by cutting a rope in half. "Mess up, you little brat," Deborah whispered.

The boy waved his hand over the rope. It was still in two pieces. He looked puzzled, but he made another joke. The crowd laughed, but not as hard as before.

It got worse. Every trick went wrong. Toward the end, even Deborah felt sorry for him. But, as she was called on stage to take her trophy for first place, she stopped thinking about him at all.

In her hands, the trophy was like a bowl that could hold unlimited dreams and hopes. It was hers, and she had earned it. Her vow, though bruised, remained unbroken.

As she left the stage, she saw him again. His top hat was on the floor, crushed under his foot. His bow tie had been flung across the room. He looked up at her and said, "You just won 'cause you're a girl." His mother was not in sight. Deborah figured she was probably off on another errand for her little darling.

"Girls aren't magicians," the boy told her.

Deborah bent down close to him and put her mouth next to his ear. "That's going to change," she said quietly. She hesitated, glanced around, then said one thing more. "And you forgot something, you stupid little boy. Maybe you think girls aren't magicians. But even a silly little brat like you must know that some girls are witches. I couldn't fix the mess you made of my equipment. I'm not that powerful yet. But making someone turn clumsy—that's not hard at all. I could do that when I was three. I can do even more now." She touched his lips with her right forefinger and whispered a final word.

"Silence."

Then she laughed and walked away.

She almost felt pity for him. Without looking back, she knew he was standing there with his mouth open and his face frozen in surprise. For the moment, the world would be spared from having to hear him. His voice would come back in an hour or two. As for his clumsiness, Deborah suspected it might last a while longer. Eventually, it might wear off. But, for the moment, it looked like some boys weren't destined to be magicians, either.

RYAN AND ANGEL IN THE GREEN ROOM, A HEAVENLY FANTASY; OR, THE ULTIMATE IN HIGH-STAKES TESTING

{ MEL GLENN }

Visions of the hereafter always tweak the curiosity. Mel Glenn uses his unique style of storytelling—free verse—to present a vision of approaching the "Pearly Gates" and gaining admission to Heaven.

Death is the ultimate fantasy.

Who has not wondered and worried over what happens when we die?

Ryan Dority, a typical teen, a student at Tower High School, hits a tree at fifty miles an hour. His companion is trapped in the car, relatively unhurt, while he is thrown clear of the vehicle and is severely injured. He is rushed to the hospital, where he is presently being operated upon, his life hanging between the tree of life and the tree of death.

His guide is Angel, a Hispanic employee who will guide Ryan through his initial intake, a three-hour exam that is the ultimate in high-stakes testing, a celestial SAT, if you will.

This interchange between Ryan and Angel takes place in the Green Room, a huge studio that is the staging area prior to meeting the Host who will decide Ryan's final fate.

No doubt, many people have an idea of what lies Beyond. Who is to say that the Green Room is not the way it plays out? What is your idea of what lies Beyond? What is your vision, your fantasy, your destiny?

THE CAR
What am I doing?
Cut it out, Ryan.
Why?
Look at the road.
I'd rather look at you.
Ryan, stop it.
Come on, Donna, you know you love me.
Not right now I don't. Watch the road.
Okay, no sweat, I know what I'm doin'.
Ryan, please! Slow down.
I know what I'm doin'.
Watch out! Ryan, Oh, God! We're gonna cra—

ANGEL RAMIREZ, THE GREEN ROOM
Oh, you're up, in a manner of speaking, of course.
You can call me Ramirez, pal.
Welcome to the Green Room.
You do know what a Green Room is, don't you?
You've seen talk shows on TV, haven't you?
Relax, we not due onstage yet.
Eat something meanwhile, a nice spread, no?

I went out and got some of your favorite foods,
pizza with anchovies, you like that, right?
Feel free to watch any of the monitors.
Your life will be shown on all channels, and in high
    definition.
Then when I give the signal,
you'll follow me and walk out onto the set
where the Host will talk to you, and when he's finished,
you exit stage left, simple really.
That's all you have to do—and then, the rest is Eternity.
Watch the cables. Where are you, you ask?
Think of this as a giant TV studio.
See the screens there? We can zoom in on anyone,
    anytime, anywhere.
I know what you're thinking—Big Brother,
but we don't interfere all that much in the affairs of men.
People give us far too much credit for intervention.
I see you are fascinated by all these monitors, check them
    out.

RYAN DORITY
Hey, Ramirez, is it? Hold on a sec.
Where am I? Am I dead?
What am I supposed to do, just stand here looking at TV?
What about what I want?
Hey, man, I got stuff to do.
There are my finals and a party next week.
I plan to head down to the shore and chill.
You can't be messin' up my plans; that's so wrong.
Don't I get something like free will?

ANGEL RAMIREZ

Free will? Get you. Are you a lawyer or something?

You didn't even ask about the girl.

Yeah, Donna. You like her? You two an item?

She's gonna be all right, no thanks to you.

Your finals? Hah! Get real. We got finals of our own. Big-
    time.

Be careful to bring two number-two pencils, like they
    always tell you to do.

Me an angel? Hardly, more like a FedEx employee.

I just get to deliver the bodies, upstairs, downstairs, what-
    ever.

Just waiting for the shipping labels, you know, up or down.

You wanna know if you died? Well, pal, not yet.

Right now you're in a coma; the doctors are workin' on you
    right now.

Your heart may give out; your body may give in.

You could fall off the operating table at any moment, dead,

in a heartbeat, or for lack of one, you get what I'm sayin'?

I gotta tell you, though, wish He'd hurry up and decide.

I got my rounds to do, collecting a child in Charleston,

a woman in Washington, all by the end of what you call a
    day.

Yeah, I only work the States, eastern seaboard mostly.

Just deaths, births are a whole 'nother unit.

You, pal, are floatin' somewhere in the hammock

'tween the green tree of life and the barren tree of death.

I got a flair for the dramatic, you think?

Hey, we got music if you like, not just gospel.

I'm partial to Elvis myself

You know, right now, while we're waitin',
you could contemplate your soul,
atone for your sins, decide what activities you want to
    register for,
assuming, of course, you don't make it, and are heading
    upstairs.
You could sign up for pottery for a few centuries,
and then switch if you want something else, no sweat.
But if I were you, I'd study hard for your, or rather our,
    finals—
Call it what you will, the Mega Final, the Eternity
    Enchilada,
the Exam Book of Life or Death, to be taken at the desk
    over there.
Before that, you should line up your testimonials.
What testimonials? You're kiddin' me, right?
You in a coma or what? Sorry, I forgot; that's exactly what
    you're in.
People gotta pray over you, people you know and love.
They gotta do this *before* you take your Finals.
Got anybody who loves you? Let them step right up.
I know you loved your dog, Speed-O, your Welsh terrier,
but he doesn't count; he died, right?
Think of this as your celestials SATs, that's right, a test.
All life is a test, don't you think? But first the testimonials!
Quiet, I think I hear somebody.

LILLIAN DORITY, RYAN'S MOTHER
(TESTIMONIAL NUMBER ONE)
I always thought You were on my side, until now.

I always thought I attended mass enough times,
donated regularly to the collection plate, until now.
Doesn't it work that way? I express my belief in You,
and in return, You keep me and my family out of harm's
     way.
I do believe You exist only to give people
false hope in an indifferent universe.
I will do anything You ask, believe in You even more,
if You spare my son and return him to me.

MICHAEL DORITY, RYAN'S FATHER
(TESTIMONIAL NUMBER TWO)
Sitting in the hospital emergency room,
holding my wife's hand, she cries, "Let us pray together."
I do not tell my wife I think my son has already died.
Ryan, do you already see the bright lights of heaven?
Or is my wife's unshakable faith an illusion,
a cosmic carnival tent erected to give people a reason to
     believe,
a place to hang their spiritual hats, a rung to rest their
     pathetic hopes?
But I would accept God as father in a second,
if only He returns my son, Ryan, to me.

BILLY FARRELLY, RYAN'S BEST FRIEND
(TESTIMONIAL NUMBER THREE)
Yo, man, what's up with this coma bit?
You missin' all the action on the courts.
Word on the street has it you got banged up pretty bad,
and might never play ball again, bummer.

Hey, but whatta these docs know? They don't know
  everything.
I say you're gonna be back in the park, playin' real soon.
So, just hurry, and get back on your feet, okay?
I'm holdin' your place for the next open court.
Everyone in the park is waitin' for you.

DONNA RAE TYLER, RYAN'S GIRLFRIEND (SORTA)
(TESTIMONIAL NUMBER FOUR)
They're making me stay here overnight.
They say you're in a coma, somewhere on a different floor.
Damn it, Ryan, will you wake up?
I'm not gonna let you get away with this.
In the roller coaster of our relationship, you took me for a
  ride.
The beginning was so sweet, a slow climb to the top of the
  hill,
with hands like birds, flapping at each other.
But when the ride was over, you didn't even ask me how I
  felt,
or what the next ride would be.
It will be a while before I buy a ticket again to love,
my heart for the moment incapable of feeling, so good, so
  bad, so quickly.
I should have been smart enough to take the bus today,
  stupid me.
Because I was not thrown clear of the vehicle, does that
  mean
I will always feel tangled up in the car crash of your life?

RYAN DORITY

You satisfied? Four testimonials enough?

So, can you let me go back to my old life, maybe precrash?

The test—now? Where? Right now? Am I gonna die?

Does it count? Is there extra credit?

I'm not ready; I didn't study.

Whaddya mean, I studied my whole life for this?

If I flunk it, can I take it over?

I don't feel well. Can I leave the room?

Whaddya mean, there's no exit?

I didn't have enough time to review.

Whaddya mean He's been reviewing your life all along?

How many words do I have to write?

Will there be extra time if I can't finish?

Whaddya mean, I have all the time out of this world?

I forgot, pen or pencil? Is it hard?

Am I gonna live through this? After I do the operation?

You didn't tell me there'd be math on it.

That desk in the corner?

Okay, okay, I'm not stalling; Ramirez, bring it on.

If I ace it, I live, right?

Ryan Dority

Row 1, Seat 1

Final Examination

Question #1—Best Memory

Directions: Answer quickly, without too much thought, indicate your best memory of the past year. First thought, stream of consciousness suggested. You will be graded on clarity, honesty, and originality of thought by a distinguished panel of writers armed with red pencils and green eyeshades.

Friday afternoon, no school, at the mall, Old Navy, Banana Republic, walking around, chilling, checking out clothes, girls, watching the world pass by, cell phone ringing, describing the hot chicks, rating 1–10, out of my league, I can dream, eating pizza with anchovies, check *that* one out, a smile, a smile back, wow, more eating, ice cream, listening to my MP3 player, movie, maybe, anything good? No matter, call my friends again, buy a LeBron T-shirt, #23, could live in Modell's Sports Shop, my idea of heaven (wait, let me change that), my idea of heaven when it's time! Then going to Puppy City to buy my dog, Speed-O, stuff there all the time. I used to love playing with him, but he died.

Preliminary Response: By Judges' Panel, Canon of Dead Authors, J. Steinbeck, Chair

While we applaud the sincerity expressed, we are a bit taken aback by the *self-centeredness* of this answer. There is nothing to indicate from the above that the subject in question relates to any other concern except his own and has a most limited view of what true happiness requires, with the possible saving grace of his affection for his dog.

Question #2—Worst News, personal or not
Directions: Same as previous question, except try poetic form.

This last summer I practiced my sport,
By tirelessly running up and down the court.

All through the days I worked and strained,
Not even stopping when it began to rain.
I played endless games of half court three on three,
Praying perhaps a coach would see me.
I practiced my dribble, my cross-over, too,
I had a dream; I never got blue.
I practiced my autograph, the applause in my head.
I drained the winning shot before going to bed.
The day of the tryout I was as confident as could be.
That lasted until the coach quickly cut me.

Second Response by the Judges

Given a totally banal rhyme scheme (AABB), and a dearth of any poetic creativity, which we are prepared to overlook, we are nevertheless shocked by what subject considers upsetting news. Though he is young, and obviously immature, it is quite possible he has not studied any history at all. We wonder at the nature of his education and conclude his sense of bad news seems, at best, inconsequential.

Question #3—Parents

Directions. Same as previous question, except try letter form in which you describe *why* your parents are important to you.

To Whom It May Concern:

My parents don't hassle me too much. Sometimes my mother is kind of annoying, nagging me to wear a seat belt (It's the law, I should have listened, but how can you talk to a girl when you're all wrapped up in a seat belt?), wanting me to come home too early, or bothering me about my social life. She also gets on me about my grades, but when I tell her I'll do better next time, she backs off—until the next report card. She's okay, I guess. My father is okay, too, but is kind of quiet, does crossword puzzles.

Third Response by the Judges

Superficial love is expressed here. It is apparent that his parents are not a matter of importance to him. Nowhere above is the idea *he* could or should do something for his parents, let alone something for the good of humanity. He believes with a simple mind and heart that the world exists for him and him alone. It is a wonder to us that he really cared for Speed-O.

Question #4—Last Question

Directions: Persuasive essay in which you try to influence Final Placement. Remember, the decision of the Host is final. Proper English is preferable, as well as neat handwriting. You have fifteen minutes to complete this portion of the test. Do not turn back to previous answers.

Hey, hold up for a minute. No way this is fair. Why are you rushing me? You want to send me someplace eternal based on what I say on one exam, or even one question? I've never been good on tests, and for that you're sending me to eternity? Seventeen years. That's all you're giving me? That's all I get? Well, I am not having any of this. I want the time before the accident. I want my old life back. Before you ship me off, God knows where, I'd like to know what my rights are, my rights as a human being. (I'm still one, aren't I?) It's not fair; I want a do-over!

Fourth Response by the Judges

Considering his Permanent Record, Previous Statements, and Test Results, we conclude he manifests self-absorbed demeanor, perhaps no different from a typical teenager on the slippery cusp of adulthood. Final decision, of course, to be announced by our Host after our theological station break. Back to you, Angel. (Forward all written documents.)

ANGEL RAMIREZ
Funny how life is or isn't.
Dude steps off the curb,
and a car misses him by one inch.
Thirty seconds later, another car, another person,
he becomes roadkill.
Truck drives over a railroad crossing,
no train in sight.
It goes along its merry way.
Another truck, same crossing,
thirty seconds later, train cuts it in half.
When a race dies, or a civilization,
or even one person in a car crash,
who decides if they are on the wrong side of thirty
    seconds?
Funny, who lives, who dies,
who laughs, who cries,
who sings, who prays, who counts the days?
Who makes his mark upon the earth,
who decides what he was worth?
Who gets to choose his mortal date,
Is it accident, is it fate?

Not my job, I have no tears,
When He calls, I just say, "Here!"
And now give it up for our Host. Cue Seraphims . . .
(*applause, applause*)

HOST
Thank you, Angel, and welcome to our first guest, Ryan
    Dority, (*more applause*)
who sadly suffered the misfortune of crashing into a
    telephone pole.
Good to see you, Ryan, how are you doing? Not so good, I
    bet,
what with the doctors working on you like that.
Sorry, it won't be much longer now,
but we first have to deal with some administrative matters.
How religious are you?
Not that it is necessarily a requirement for heaven these
    days,
not like what it was in medieval times.
You don't go to church every Sunday do you?
Why should I bestow My benevolence on you?
Do you even believe in Me?
Speak up, young man. Now is the time to defend yourself.

RYAN DORITY
That's just the point!
I don't know if I believe in you.
You may be real, I don't know.
You could be just another icon on the screen over there.
I can't tell you what I believe in; I'm only seventeen.

If my life sucks, it's the only life I have. I can't help who I am.
Couldn't you just send me back, pretend this never
    happened,
place me in time before the car, before the accident?
I promise I won't cause any trouble.
I'll drive more carefully, I swear.
I'll even go to church more regularly.
I'll sign any papers you have.
Please let me live. I don't have anything else.

HOST
We do not need any papers signed.
We do not need any loyalty oaths taken.
I thank you for your honest prayers, Ryan,
and state for the record that your present condition,
is not part of My plan, global or local.
Contrary to accepted belief,
I do not control or see everything.
Regrettably, there have been quite a few examples
in the course of planets, and in the affairs of men,
that have escaped My observation,
particularly in the last century, concerning world wars,
with the slaughter of millions, especially the children.
But for now, let's look at your record, shall we?
Let's examine subordinate reports, final exams,
advocacy statements, not to mention your impassioned plea.
Know that I ultimately understand nearly everything,
allowing for some things are just pure chance.
I'm thinking, given the nature of your less than stellar per-
    formance,

it is quite impossible to render a conclusive verdict at this
    time.
So, therefore, reprising my role as Ultimate Teacher, and
    noting
there is little benign indifference on my part I decree that
Angel Ramirez is to accompany you
as you are assigned to inhabit other lives, all teenagers,
so you can learn, grow, and see how other people live.
I have them all picked out:
Darius, a young Afro-American; Irina, A Russian
    schoolgirl;
Jorge, a Hispanic premed student; Ibrahim, a Muslim
    young man;
Steven, a Jewish theological student; Jennie, a Chinese
    violinist; and
Lindsay, a seventeen-year-old girl from Nevada who likes
    flowers.
You were going to be an aluminum siding salesperson, and
I don't think the world needs another one. So—
in terms of your here and now, I am sorry to say,
I am going to have to declare you Officially Dead.
I know this isn't what you wanted to hear,
but consider yourself fortunate, more fortunate than most.
You get your "do-over," just not with your own life.
You will get to decide upon, and settle into your new life,
    one of the above.
Come on, now, let's get going. You have a lot to learn about
    being
a man, a woman, a human being, Darius first.
Hopefully, you will come to see the call of compassion,

the mercies of the heart in these other lives.
And hopefully, you will see that you are to be
allowed on earth again to make the world a better place for
    others.
Also, because you were good to him,
I am returning Speed-O to you. Only now,
he's a St. Bernard, yes, we do dogs, too.
This is my decision, final and irrevocable.
The show is now over, thank you, cast and crew.
See you all soon, feel free to tune in anytime.
Good luck and My speed.

LILLIAN DORITY, RYAN'S MOTHER
You must have had your reasons.
You must have figured my son
would be better off with You.
But You must know that ending his life,
has ended mine as well.
No, I will not leave the Church.
No, I will not stop my prayers to You.
I didn't think I had asked for much.
For others, You have parted the seas, and made miracles.
For others, You have done wonders and have given life.
You must have had your reason for taking him away.
You just forgot to tell me why.

ANGEL RAMIREZ—FINAL VOICE-OVER
Yo, man, I'm beat.
I gotta put in for some R and R.
This one wasn't easy, man, all that surgery and stuff, ugh.

But I gotta agree with Him.
Look at Ryan, I mean Darius.
He's out on the courts, chilling with his pals.
And look over there, the St. Bernard
is just sitting there, watching them play.
Billy Farrelly thinks Darius looks kind of familiar,
but can't quite put his finger on it.
He's got a good shot to make himself and others happy,
a good shot to make himself feel really alive.
Aww . . . what more can you ask for now?
Basketball, friends, and a faithful dog.
What, you're sending me back, where?
Hope it's not a car crash again.
What—the shipping labels are here—already?

THE YOUNGEST ONE

{ NANCY SPRINGER }

A teenage girl, a warty neighbor, a blue-eyed toad, an alcoholic mother, two irresponsible older brothers, a long-gone father, and Shakespeare. Nancy Springer connects these dissimilar characters to create a most imaginative tale.

"Good morning, Jessica," called the squatty old woman who always sat on the porch of number 321.

What's so good about it? Jessie wanted to scream, her mood as heavy as the backpack hanging from her arm as she trudged toward school. *There's nothing to eat, not even a slice of bread, and Mom's passed out on the sofa again.* But she forced a small smile, and replied, "Morning."

"Jessica." Leaning toward her, Warty beckoned her closer. Warty was what the kids in the nabe called the old woman because there were bumps on her face, each with a single thick white hair sticking out like a cat's whisker. Warty's hunched body looked kind of lumpy too, under her polyester dress, and it bulged like a bean bag over the edges of her chair. Most of the kids called her names, laughing at her to her face.

But Jessie never wanted to hurt anyone, especially not a bent-over old woman who could barely walk. Her mood was so bad she wished she could ignore old Warty, but that would be mean. So, stepping off the sidewalk, she stood at Warty's gray, unpainted porch railing.

The old woman's knobby hand hovered in the air as she fixed Jessie with a stare. "Are you studying Shakespeare in school right now, Jessica?" Those old eyes, faded blue, almost white, seemed suddenly so bright that facing Warty was like being caught in front of a pair of halogen headlights on high beam.

"Um, yeah," Jessie stammered. "Yes." Eighth-graders had to read Shakespeare, written in the sixteenth century and having *sooo* much to do with Jessie's life in a low-rent row house on Railroad Street.

"Which play?"

"Um . . ." Jessie had to think. "*As You Like It.*"

The old woman nodded once, decisively, and her crooked hand settled in her lap. "Read it closely and pay attention," she ordered.

"Um, sure. All right." Sensing herself dismissed, Jessie stepped back and kept walking toward school, though she didn't feel like going. What was the use? With Dad run off, no clue where, and Mom drunk or maybe stoned too, and Jarod and Jason staying out all night instead of helping the way older brothers ought to, what was the use of anything?

Jessie went to school only because she was hungry. She didn't have lunch money, but one of her friends would lend her a dollar, or share with her, or something.

As You Like It? Whatever. Jessica didn't like it, especially not taking up the whole English period. She did not pay attention.

Lunch was fish sticks and cornbread. Lots of kids didn't like it, so Jessica ate what they didn't want. After lunch she skipped out.

She did not want to go home—what for? But she couldn't think of anywhere else she wanted to go, either. So she wandered the streets. Slow, random, eyes on the gray pavement—

Something the color of a UPS truck squatted right in the middle of the sidewalk in front of her. Lumpy. At first Jessie thought it was a pile left by a very large dog.

But before she could say "Ew!" she saw that it was alive and looking at her. Motionless, but watching her.

She exclaimed, "A *toad*?"

What would a toad be doing in the city? Jessie had never seen one before. But there sat one about the size and shape of a roadkilled softball. A toad. Not a frog. Even a city girl ought to know the difference, Jessie considered; a frog would have been all sleek like a biker in leathers, not sloppy and bumpy like it was made of warts.

"What are you doing here, toad?" Jessie hunkered down to face it as if she were talking with a child.

The toad just stared at her.

Weird. Its eyes were blue. A way, way pale blue.

"Are your eyes supposed to be that color?" Jessie asked. "I mean, what do I know? I never met a toad before. Aren't you kind of big for a toad?" It also seemed weird that the toad was not afraid of her. Not hopping away. Its front feet turned inward, half hidden under its belly, like crooked little hands. Its hind feet sprawled at ease on the concrete.

Jessie started to feel worried about it.

"You can't just sit there, funny face," she told the toad. "Some butthead will do something to you." Some kids in her nabe had got hold of a turtle once, and pounded it with rocks until it broke open. Jessie had tried to stop them, but it was like trying to stop Mom from drinking, no way. A bunch of kids had grabbed her by the arms and made her watch while the other ones killed the turtle. Remembering, Jessie felt sick.

"Get out of here, toad." Standing up, Jessie nudged it gently with her foot, feeling like she didn't want to touch it with her hands. She'd heard that touching a toad would give you warts, and while she didn't really believe that, the toad did look kind of gross. Anyhow, she didn't know whether toads had teeth, and what if it bit her?

Shoved by her toe, the toad didn't even blink. Maybe toads couldn't blink. It didn't move, either, just sat there with its fat yellowish belly spread like a soft suction cup on the sidewalk.

"Move, toad!" Jessie inserted her sneaker toe under its hind end.

The toad didn't budge.

"Come on!" She tried using her foot like a lever to get the toad moving.

Contentedly it sat the way she'd propped it.

"Oh, why do I care?" Stepping away, Jessie turned to keep on walking wherever she was going.

Nowhere.

While the toad sat where some creep with size-thirteen Nikes could stomp it flat.

Jessie shook her head, rolled her eyes, and bent over. She whispered, "Yuck." When she straightened, she held the toad

in both hands in front of her. Spread across her cupped palms,
the toad felt flabby, clammy, and not real likely to move. Kind
of like a big cold fried egg, only squishier.

"Sweet are the uses of adversity;
Which like the toad, ugly and venomous,
Wears yet a precious jewel in his head. . . ."

Dozing through English class the next day, Jessie sat up suddenly to listen. Toad? Hidden under her bed at home, sitting
in some moist dirt in a cardboard box, was a toad, and Jessie
wondered what to feed it. She had brought it various wormy
things she'd found underneath loose bricks, but the toad had
shown no interest in the creepy-crawlies.

"What does Shakespeare mean by this?" the teacher was
asking. "What is 'adversity'?"

No one wanted to answer, of course, but eventually it came
out that adversity was sort of adverse weather in a person's life.
Like bad luck, or hard times.

"Now, in Shakespeare's era, people believed toads were hor-
rible, ugly animals associated with witches, poisonous to
touch," the teacher said as if she thought anybody cared. "But
they also believed that often bad things carried their own cure.
In a way we still do believe that. For instance, people still say
'fight fire with fire' or 'hair of the dog that bit you.'"

This wasn't helping Jessie any. She started to lose interest.

". . . considered the toad venomous, yet at the same time
they believed that inside the toad's head was a jewel, a precious
gemstone. And they believed that this toadstone provided a
magical cure for poison."

Sure. Whatever.

"So by this simile, Shakespeare is saying that, in a hidden way, hard times can be a blessing for us."

If that teacher thought that whatsit, adversity, was such a good thing, she ought to try having a departed father, a drunken mother, and disappearing brothers. Jessie tuned out.

Home from school, Jessie found no one there, as usual. No father, no mother, no brothers. But, letting her book bag drop to the kitchen floor, she reminded herself that there *was* a big peaceable toad, unless . . . It never seemed to move, like, maybe there was something wrong with its legs, but what if it had remembered how to hop? What if it had gotten out of the box and gone away?

Taking the stairs two at a time, Jessie ran up to her room, lunged to her knees, and eased the box out from under the bed.

Squatty, lumpy, and serene, the toad gazed back at her with pale blue-white eyes.

Jessie sighed with relief, smiling. "Hi, toad!" Gently, grasping it around its bulgy middle with both hands, Jessie lifted it out of the box. Its flabbiness no longer felt yucky to her. Cupping it in both palms, she lifted it to her eye level, and asked, "Are you okay? Did you eat anything?"

The toad just sat there as if in an armchair, its crooked little hands resting on her thumbs.

"What do you want me to bring you, pepperoni pizza? What do toads eat?"

Not that she expected any answer. But she felt better having something, anything, to talk to.

"Maybe Mom went for food. Whatever she brings home, I'll give you some. *If* she brings any."

Steadily the toad met her gaze with its freaky cloud-and-sky eyes.

"Are you a Shakespeare toad? I know you're not, like, venomous, but do you have a precious stone—"

With a squeak Jessie stopped talking, for in that moment the toad's eyes focused on her in a way they hadn't before: intense, vehement, bright, so bright Jessie couldn't see anything else; it was like being caught in front of a pair of halogen headlights. Just like—

But even as she thought where she had seen such eyes before, she felt the toad's dumpy weight leave her hands. Not hop away. Just leave. As she gawked, blinking in disbelief, she saw the ghost of a toad, then, blink, the dried-out mummy of a dead toad older than Shakespeare, then the feather-light skeleton of a toad, and finally, all in a moment, a shining, weightless blue-white jewel.

The jewel stayed.

But Jessie's right hand closed around it, without recognition, as she bolted to her feet with a cry. A terrible thought had taken hold of her like a clenched fist. Downstairs she ran so fast she almost fell, and out the door, and up the street toward number 321. "Mrs. Warty!" she yelled, panting, trying not to cry. "Mrs., um . . ." She didn't know her elderly neighbor's proper name. "Are you still there?"

Yes. Now she could see the old woman. On her porch. Hunchbacked, she seemed to sag in her chair. . . . Was she alive?

Rushing up to the porch, Jessie cried, "Please, are you . . . are you . . ." She couldn't get the words out.

The old woman's bright, pale eyes lifted to look at her. "What's the matter?"

"Are you *all right*?"

"Of course I'm all right." The old woman leaned forward, peering. "Are you?"

"I, um, I don't know!"

"You have a good heart, Jessica. Always concerned for others before yourself." With a quirk of her rumpled face that might have been a smile, Warty added, "I'm fine. Toads are simple."

What . . . toad . . . old Warty really did know all about it? Jessie had to hang on to the weathered gray porch railing for support, trying to get past a dizzy feeling.

"Good thing you weren't reading *King Lear*," the old woman remarked. "Or *Hamlet*, or anything with crazy people or apparitions. Then it would have been harder. You know, Shakespeare was a friend of mine, and I helped him with the three witches in *Macbeth*."

Jessie understood only a little of this, which was still enough to start her trembling.

"Jessica, you have nothing to be afraid of," said the old woman softly. "You know, when the wicked stepmother drives the children away, it's always the youngest one, the humble one, kind to old people and animals, who returns with the treasure."

Still dazed, Jessie struggled for an answer. "I, um, I don't have a wicked stepmother. . . ."

"That's just code for what these days they call dysfunctional. Now, let me see what you have in your hand."

Eyes widening as she remembered, Jessie lifted her right hand and opened it.

On her palm shone what appeared to be a very large pearl, blue-tinged, but not round. Smooth and lustrous yet irregular, its shape resembled that of her recent squatting, brown friend.

"A perfect toadstone. Beautiful." The old woman's eyes glowed like the gem in Jessie's hand. "Do you understand what you are to do with it, Jessica?"

"Um, sell it for money to get some food?"

"No. Certainly not. Now, young lady, think. I told you to pay attention in Shakespeare class."

It was a long wait for Mom to come home.

Even after midnight, Jessie remained perched on the edge of the sofa. In the dark, as if she were on a stakeout. Too tense to lean back, too nervous to watch TV or do homework or even eat, although after she had come back from talking with Mrs. Warty she had found a loaf of warm brown bread and a wedge of yellow cheese on the table.

So far, even as bad as things had been, Mom had always come home at night. She couldn't pass out somewhere else *now*. She had to show up soon. Please.

Waiting, begging the air to make her mother come home to her, Jessica cuddled the toadstone in her hands until its blue-white form became as warm as her blood.

Finally, must have been around two or three o'clock in the morning, she heard the sound of feet dragging outside, an unsteady key clawing in the dark.

Stiff from sitting so long, Jessie got up, flipped on the front light and opened the door.

Wobbling and unfocused, her mother faced her without seeming to recognize her for a moment. Then she said blurrily, "What you doing home? You kids 'spose to be in school."

"That's during the daytime, Mom." It hurt Jessie's heart to see her mother this way. Usually she would have been avoiding Mom, curled up in bed with her eyes shut tight. But tonight, taking hold of her mother by one elbow, Jessie guided her inside and shut the door. Mom staggered toward the sofa, but Jessie swung her around and sat her in a chair instead.

"Whatcha doing?" Mom slurred. "Didjer Dad get back from bowling yet?"

"Oh, is *that* where he went." On one knee in front of her mother, Jessica held out the toadstone like an offering. "Mom, look."

In the dim room, the toadstone glimmered with its own blue-white light.

Mom's wandering glance caught on the glowing gem. Jessie saw Mom's bleary eyes widen, focusing, and she saw a freaky kind of understanding in that stare, as if Mom knew what the toadstone was for even though she could not possibly ever have seen one before. Mrs. Warty had said it would be that way.

Mrs. Warty had said Mom had a choice: to reach out and take the toadstone, or not.

And whichever way Mom chose, that was the way it had to be.

Jessie found herself holding her breath.

"Oh," said Mom uncertainly. "Oh, weird. Kind of ugly, kind of booful. Zat for me?"

"If you want it."

With a fumbling hand Mom reached toward the stone. But she hesitated before she touched it.

Jessie had to bite her lip to keep quiet. If she tried to tell Mom what to do, it would ruin everything.

Mom's hand floated like a butterfly in the air for a moment that seemed like forever . . . but then softly alighted on the toadstone. Mom's unsteady fingers curled around the gem. She lifted it, held it in front of her face.

Jessie started to breathe again.

And in that moment Jessie's mother sat up straight, steady. Her eyes cleared. "Jessica," she said, her voice no longer slurred. "Jessie!" She leaned over to hug her daughter, pulling Jessie up off the floor and into her lap like a little girl. "Jessie, Jessie, Jessie, how did you do it?" She hugged her daughter. "Is this really for me?"

"Of course." Suddenly feeling all choked up as if she might cry, Jessie couldn't say much.

"I'll carry it always," Mom told her. "I'll get us some groceries first thing tomorrow, then start looking for a job. What are you doing up so late? You need to get your sleep so you can pay attention in school."

Jessie whispered, "Um, no more drinking or drugs?"

"No more," said Mom in a strong, sure voice. "Why would I? Jessica, that stuff is nothing but poison."

BASEBALL IN IRAQ (BEING THE TRUE STORY OF THE GHOST OF GUNNERY SERGEANT T. J. McVEIGH)

{ JOHN H. RITTER }

John H. Ritter tells us a ghost story with a twist. The ghost is an American villain, who seems to be doing right in the realm of the passed. His job is to debrief the newly dead. Ritter keeps the reader wondering where this is leading.

He wakes up every morning swimming in the purest form of sadness, trappedness, drabness one can imagine. This is not the way I want to live my life, he mutters. Around him are the rubble middens of brick and cinder block, painted plaster chunks and stone. Corpses lie about, children and adults. The neighborhood is in ruin, its streets boulder-pocked by bomb-blast debris. He scans a papyrus scroll, then glances up again.

Overnight, simple, modest Iraqi homes have been shaken apart, blasted apart, and now sit roofless, heartless, their yards littered with broken timbers and crumbled block piled upon handmade artifacts.

Here he spies an empty wooden picture frame, half buried in mud; there, the splintered top of a hand-carved cedar tea table; and underfoot, a girl's black Bukhnag head scarf trimmed in gold lace. Drifting past, eyeing the sight, Gunnery Sgt. T. J. McVeigh twists his mouth into a mourner's clench.

By now there is no sobbing. He hears only low moans, which occasionally build into wails ending in shrieks, not unlike the sound he imagines a child might make if someone were to rip away a fingernail.

Nearby wanders a woman who, with an infant at her breast, weeps as she pokes and jabs a stick into the ruins of her home.

He wakes up every morning, folds his hands, and prays for rain. Anything to wash all this away. No one listens, as far as he can tell.

Floating toward the chopper wreckage, he spots the American airman he will serve this day. He tucks the scroll away. And the angelic voices in his head begin to sing.

(E minor / 4/4/ up-tempo blues)
Em   Am
Messenger man says go on down and choose up sides
Em   Am
Place your bets you Capulets and let 'em ride
Em   Am   Em
Battle like a pack o' dogs til you die,
            G   D   Em
because only the lonely survive.

Who are you? the fallen man asks, amid the tangled fuselage of an Apache helicopter.

T. J. focuses on his face, young, maybe eighteen, nineteen, bloody, intense. I'm the InDoc. He kneels alongside. T. J.'s eyes roam the split torso, the ragged edges of his missing leg.

You a doctor? the young man asks.

No. T. J. lifts and cradles the man close. But you're in good hands. You'll see.

The airman strains to rise up and look around. What happened?

Looks of it, an RPG.

I'll be damned. Don't remember a thing.

After a moment, the airman closes his eyes and lets his head fall back into T. J.'s arm. Tikrit? the kid strains to ask.

Yes.

You army?

T. J. nods. Was. Out there. With an upward jaunt of his head, he indicates the vast desert beyond. I was a gunnery sergeant on a Bradley, picking off ragheads in the desert.

Yeah? The kid softens his face. Any luck?

T. J. does not answer.

Well, to my mind, bombs are better, says the airman. You don't really have to go eyeball to eyeball with anybody. One time, west side of Baghdad, I heard they blew up 313 of 'em in a bomb shelter. His cherubic face surrenders to a smirk. Now, that's irony. Bombs wasting a bomb shelter.

This is not really a matter I am terribly interested in.

No, me either. The strain in his voice grows stronger. Collateral damage, as they say. When in the course of human events and all that.

T. J. follows the flight of two sparrows circling and darting high above the street. He feels the young helicopter gunner's eyes search his face, the natural progression of a trudging soul.

Am I dead? he asks.

The question puts life back into T. J.'s face. Yes, he says.

Rooster crows at the morning sun. The tall bird crosses by the kitchen window. Aye, Sair-gent McVeigh, he calls. His Irish brogue drips from every word. Topo' the morn to ya. I'm off to close me book, lad. So who would you be liking in the fifth race?

T. J. grins. That three-legged horse named Why Old Bill. And you?

T'ardly helps to worry off on it, says Rooster. Steroids, you know, in every horse.

What's it coming to?

What I've been a sayin, lad.

T. J. drifts off through the back wall looking for eggs. In the dust storm of his electrified mind, he hears the children's chorus again, girls and boys. They're singing the next verse of his song.

(as before . . . and throughout)

Grow up, go to school, play the soldier's game,
do a hitch, duck a pitch, sayin' who's to blame?
grow old, turn cold, drink red rain,

an' when the cop says, kid, now, whataya sayin'?
you tell 'im plain, you're sayin' you're insane,
ever since you hopped that black gold train,
an' a thought got shot right through your brain
that only the lonely survive.

T. J. strikes a match, fires up the kettle, scrapes the grease off the pan. He could be anywhere and do what he does. In the past. Into the future, certainly. Now at least, he's in the house of his youth. He resumes the InDoc.

How did you grow up?

How? The airman shrugs. Normal. I guess. He sits upright on a bench at the pale oaken table, his back against the kitchen wall. Parents got divorced. So I lived with my mom and everything. But, you know. His head knife-wobbles slightly on his short neck.

T. J. nods. I lived with my dad. We hunted. We fished. Played some ball. You do any of that?

Some. I had friends who would. Baseball buddies. I played a lot of baseball.

T. J. raises his gaze to indicate the kitchen they are in. Scanning the light yellow cabinets, the cream-colored square-tiled countertop and backsplash, the multipaned, double-hung window with tied-back curtains on one side and Rooster's open window on the other. We lived right here. This house. Upstate New York. He shuffles inside a drawer for a fork.

How'd I get here?

I like to bring guys here the first day. Home-cooked meal and all.

The airman hums. Been a while.

It has.

Leaning forward, the airman focuses on T. J.'s eyes. This ain't heaven, is it?

Get asked that a lot, says T. J. He fork-whips the eggs into a lather, then pours them into the black skillet, which erupts in sizzle and steam. Don't really believe in heaven. Never have. Or hell, for what it's worth, except the one out there. He waves the silver spatula with a swordsman's flair toward the side window. Immediately, the true image of a war zone appears through the panes. Urban setting. Lightning blasts. Mortar rocket concussions. The kitchen walls and floor quake in sympathy.

'Course, I always said, T. J. shouts above it all, if there is a hell, soulfully speaking, and I was goin' to it, then at least I'd be in good company. I mean, with all those fighter pilots who also had to bomb innocents to win the war. He watches the kid's reaction to that loaded declaration.

The airman lowers his head. We don't see it like that, sir, he calls. Out there, in the chopper, it's kill or be killed. You do what you have to do, but those high-flying bombardiers are as almighty accurate as humanly possible, sir.

I don't disagree, shouts T. J. He lowers the window blind and the room quiets. But I also know that I never killed anyone in self-defense. I saw 'em, I shot 'em. Sometimes from a mile away.

The airman pushes his hands straight out across the table. We undertook a broad action, Sergeant, in order to inject a certain level of fear into the general population on our way to extracting a certain menace from that population we saw as very capable of someday doing just what you're talking about—attacking us from the sky. Over *our* land. We all know what they can do, sir.

That I do, says T. J. I wasn't there, but as I recall, they mustered up nineteen men to stage an hour-long attack on Manhattan one September morning, several years ago. You're talking about that.

A massively deadly attack, sir.

Right. And this response—years upon years of bullets and bombs and bloodshed, the incessant killing of a hundred thousand innocents—you feel certain that'll prevent the next hour-long attack on Manhattan?

The kid rotates a fist against his palm. Yes, sir.

Street corner perky merry Magdalenes
sing to the church-borne war machine
servicin' servicemen behind the scenes
while Pokémon trainers now in their teens
sync the songs an' mime their dreams
but no matter how they make it seem,
only the lonely survive.

How long have you been dead, sir?

The sergeant takes a long, deep breath, then lets it out. I suppose I should know. He glances up at the dented tin Coca-Cola clock on the wall. Let me guess. Not long. The war before this one, I think. I lose track of chronology like crazy these days. Same place, though, pretty much. This gulf, this desert. I was sent home, actually. But I never made it out.

The airman drums his palms on the tabletop. How is it? he asks.

This? Being dead? T. J. lifts the pan, slopping sausage grease over the eggs. You adapt. You adjust. I mean, what else can you do? It's part of life. He pauses a moment to stare at his stainless image caught in the reflection of a knife. But sometimes, airman, in the graylight of dawn, I grow a sadness inside that makes me want to fall on my sword. I want to erase myself from the constant and brutal surrender of hope I see out there. He flips the scramble and stirs. That ought to make you laugh.

Laugh, sir?

Well, the thought of a man who is already dead wanting to kill himself, has, I think, some inherent humor in it, eh? Hearing no reply, he slams the spatula against the stovetop. It does to a real man, blast it!

The airman does not flinch. It has irony, sir.

T. J. leans a hip against the stove. I suppose it does, he says. At any rate, I'm InDoc now. It's what I do. Get you new boys oriented and on your way. He chops into the scramble, stirs it, then brings the pan to the table.

So that's what you do? You debrief the newly dead? Settle us in or something?

I try. He dishes the sausage and eggs onto a white plate.

You must've lived a good life, sir. To be able to do this. You must've cared for people an awful lot.

I cared, T. J. answers. That I did.

The kid waits for T. J. to finish serving. So what happens next?

Next, I want you to tell me something. He takes the empty pan back to the stove.

Tell you what?

The first thought you thought when you knew you were dead. And that you weren't within gunshot of the Promised Land. T. J. returns with a stack of toast and jam and sits.

The airman shrinks noticeably, his shoulders pinch forward. I know what you're getting at. I thought about it. How I managed my life. My sins and—and if I ever tried to make amends. Because I did. Whenever I saw I'd done something wrong, I usually made the effort to make things right again. He takes a bite of eggs. Way I see myself now, I see myself about even. If that's what you wanna know.

Tell me one sin. The one on top.

On top? Geez, I don't know. He stops his fork in midair and faces away. Getting Mandy pregnant, I guess. My girlfriend. His eyes stay distant. But I never wanted her to get the abortion. I fought against that.

Yes, I know. But her parents decided.

The young man lowers his fork. When he turns back again to his plate, his gaze doesn't rise above the fork.

You know my life, he says. You know all about me, don't you? He gets no answer. Okay, then. So why are you doing this, having me confess all this, if you already know? He rises slowly, stands, and paces to the window, crossing his arms so that each hand cups an elbow. Show it to me, then, he says. Show me out the window the one that's on top.

Open it for yourself, says T. J. It's okay. You're allowed.

The airman stands frozen a long while, wavering. Finally, he grasps the bottom of the white blind, tugs, and lets go. The dense cotton blind snaps up and rolls into its case. He stares into the scene, one he knows well. God, this is so awful. His teeth clamp his bottom lip. He sucks in a breath. That's me and that's Korch, my pilot. In those Apaches, you're just a two-man crew. That day we were offering support to ground troops. They'd set up a roadblock. Word from command was that anyone rolling up to those roadblocks was armed and dangerous. In one twenty-four-hour period, we killed over thirty civilians in vehicles that rolled up too fast or rolled past. We just lit 'em up. But when our guys went to pull the corpses out of the cars, they never found any weapons. These people were just your everyday civilians—whole families sometimes—trying to leave the city. They'd just been too scared or too confused to stop.

The airman pulls the window blind shut. That's enough. I remember it all. He breathes out, at last. That was—that was the time we spotted this Iraqi kid, about my age, running across the sand. He had no weapon, but he'd been in the car, so he was a legit target. Korch swooped in, and I blew one of his arms completely off. Shattered his legs. He flipped and rolled and ended up on his back. Bloody sand all in his wounds. We started to pull up. But there was this one moment when he just looked at me—I mean, those Apaches, they can get in close—and he looked up at me with these eyes—eyes that talked. Eyes that said, Look what you did. *Look at what you did to me.* For what? And then we just flew off. Left him there. You really couldn't do much anyway, except, you know, pray.

The soldier slumps and cracks a beer
spins and shoots his shadow outta fear
sayin' it's awfully cold up here
I wish you'd get me a volunteer
while I just sort of disappear,
I'm so tired of this career,
where only the lonely survive.

Rooster trots up to the open window. Ahoy, Sair-gent! This time he rests his burnt-red elbows on the sill, leans in, and holds his head sideways to take a full gander at the airman. And who's this you've brought to your breakfast board? A fine young strapper, by the looks.

T. J. walks from the stove into closer range of the feathery old coot. That he is, he whispers, adopting Rooster's brogue. But I've need to inquire, wouldya judge him as being a good one or bad?

Rooster tilts his huge head. His full, red crown plops off to the side. Well, now, Teej. 'Taint so much a matter of good nor bad as it is left or right. Looks mighty young. A candidate for InDoc, is he?

Nay, says T. J. I'm thinkin' a Guardsman.

Garrreds-mun, is it? Well, in that case. Rooster widens his eye, giving the airman one more head-to-toe. Let's look for reason in him.

My thoughts as well, says T. J. Says he's a sportsman. Baseball.

Aye, but can he see and grasp what's what with not many a clue? Rooster clucks to clear his throat and calls inside. Who do ya like in the Series, son? Boston or them Yanks?

The kid sits tall and faces Rooster. Red Sox, he says.

Would you be wanting to place a greenback or two behind the Fenwaylians, then?

The airman stiffens. No, sir. I don't gamble.

Aye, and a fine stand that is. Rooster lowers his voice. Eh, he's got the feist and fire, Teej.

My thoughts, again.

And a gut for what's what, if you follow with my drift.

T. J. winks. I lie easy in the tide, sir.

Returning to the table with another fry pan of eggs and sausage, T. J. fills the airman's plate, then his own, and sits.

I've done other things similar, the airman says. But that was one I'll never forget. I wasn't raised like that.

You'll forget, says T. J., with calm assurance. Forgetting comes with remembrance. You see, most people never do what they believe in. They just do what they want and hope someday to repent. So, go back to that instant, friend, when your eyes met his.

The airman breathes slowly, his head hangs. Why am I here, sir? he asks. What good is this? You say there's no heaven, there's no hell, except out there—wherever *there* is. Why am I here, then? Why don't you just send me back outside—straight to hell? What do you want me to do?

I want you to eat, says T. J. He taps his fork on the airman's plate. Eat up. We'll talk later.

They eat. The plates empty and they fill again. And again. T. J. enjoys seeing the airman load his fork with meat and eggs and wash down his jellied toast with coffee and milk. He cooks up and dishes him a last helping, setting his own plate aside. He turns his chair crooked to the table and faces the blinded window.

So, why are you here, you ask. Well, in part, you're here for me.

Sir?

T. J. bends forward, placing his arms on his knees. When I saw what they let us get away with in the first Gulf War, I remember having my doubts about what real good we were doing over there. He rises to open the window blind revealing a Bradley fighting vehicle chasing down and firing at fleeing soldiers over half a mile away.

The airman glances up, but does not speak.

That's me, says T. J., in the Bradley—I'm guessing 1992. Anyway, I was deemed a model soldier. They awarded me the Bronze Star, among other medals. Out of two hundred soldiers in my platoon, I was the first one to make sergeant. I was the top marksman, too. In fact, I was the best damned soldier a lot of people had ever seen, and they told me so, over and over again.

Oh, so, that's why I'm in front of you. The perfect guy gets to tear down the shoddy gunner.

T. J. stares back. As I said, I was a gunner, too—gunnery sergeant, trained in explosives, the whole nine yards. And just before I left, they invited me to join Special Forces—the Green Berets.

I wouldn't doubt it.

Well, I would. That is, I did. My doubts grew so big, that even though I passed all the initial screenings, I realized I couldn't do anything but leave. So I got out of the army and went on home. Came right here. Physically, I was home. But the truth is, I never made it back.

I don't understand.

T. J. sighs. Nobody does, at first. Let's put it this way. The man who goes to war is never the man who returns.

There's the psychological changes, you mean.

What I mean, gunny, is that war is a vile mistress. Sorry to say, but I know from experience. War is our surrender to the adultery of bloodlust. And if you are to go forward, you must know that, too.

He motions toward the window. Outside, a woman and an infant appear, lying in the dirt, in a puddle of blood. This was in the hills of Montana, says T. J. A place called Ruby Ridge. This mother and son were shot by a U.S. government sniper as they stepped out of their cabin. And I, among many, firmly believe they were murdered.

The airman looks, but soon closes his eyes. That line does get crossed, sir.

I know, says T. J. Too often. But now I need to know this. That moment I asked you about. The moment of eye contact? Do you remember?

Yes, sir, I remember. He crosses his arms again, this time with a shudder. At the instant I looked down at that poor kid, I felt so sick, so putrid inside that I ended up swallowing my own vomit. And I thought to myself, what right did I have to come over to this person's country and kill him? The airman glares at T. J., as if demanding the answer from him. How did he ever transgress against me?

T. J. rises to blind the window. The kid sends him a dark look. The silence lasts until the kid lets his gaze fall, closing his eyes. What did *you* do? he asks. What was your moment—your top sin?

T. J. answers to the wall. After I left the army, I went on one last mission.

They called you back up?

No. This one was more personal.

In Iraq?

T. J. shakes his head. Stateside.

The airman's eyes flicker with a searcher's glint.

I only did what I was trained to do, says T. J. My mission was to let Americans know. To smell it, to taste it, like the Iraqis did every day. Like all those families did during that standoff down in Waco, Texas. To *know* what happens when you take an eighteen-year-old kid and train him to become a killer, then send him off to do your killing and let the lust of war drench his brain. Let the chemistry of his brain go haywire and frantic, and then bring him back home, cut him loose, and expect him to be okay, to be normal again. After he knows what he knows. T. J. shrugs. So I went to war against the U.S. government.

Oh, my God, says the airman. His face shows a deep grasping—one that comes with not many a clue. He points at T. J. You're the Oklahoma bomber, aren't you? You're Timothy McVeigh, who blew up the Federal Building in Oklahoma City and killed all those people.

T. J. does not blink. I am, he says. We all are.

No! The kid bolts upright, his thighs catching the table and lifting it, spilling coffee and clanging the plates and silverware. Don't put me in with guys like you! You went crazy. You killed innocent Americans who never had a chance. And that day-care center—all those little kids. He strides toward the back door, then spins. God almighty! What I did—it was nowhere close to your crime.

No? T. J. answers flatly, with words he has often used. In the eyes of the angels, he tells the airman, what you did was precisely my crime. Once you cross that line, gunny, degrees don't matter.

Degrees? You talk about degrees? What about *right and wrong?* You don't just go around blowing up innocent people. You can't just—he pauses—not in America, you can't. I mean, you can't just go and—he stops.

Shaking, he looks away and walks to the darkened window. There he stands for what seems an eternity. All alone he stands, staring, as if seeing something he'd never seen before.

Degrees don't matter, T. J. repeats. Evil is evil. That's what no one ever tells us. But I'm telling you now, my friend.

Nineteen children on the mountainside
singin' Jesus was a liberal, an' so am I
as the blackhawk barrels in from the sky
they just keep a-singin' as the bullets fly
til the very last moment when they realize
that the reason they live is the reason they die,
for only the lonely survive.

Your InDoc is over.
What? The motionless airman speaks over folded arms.
The indoctrination is complete. It's time for you to move on.

Move on? What do you mean? He turns to face T. J.

We want you to go where the need is greatest. The thought here is that you'll become a Guard.

A guard? Guarding what?

The minds of the weary. We anticipate a flood of soldiers heading back to the U.S. after this war. Some wounded, some not, but they will all have been brain addled by this war.

Wait, I won't be working with you, sir?

No, you'll be working alone—and for the living ones. As a Guard, you'll focus on one soul at a time. You'll hover above, hover close.

The airman considers the idea. I can do that, sir.

You will evaluate their challenges. Then you'll send them liberal doses of warm, generous humanitarian thoughts, based on what you now know to be true, which they can turn into hunches.

How do I do that?

You love 'em. No matter what. Won't be hard, actually. Pretty soon, they'll get a feeling—a hunch, an urge—one that is true and holy and useful for whatever problem they face.

That's it?

That's it. T. J. grins.

The airman crumples against the back wall, grinning himself. I'm a guardian angel, he says.

Yes, sir. And you'll be a damn good one.

The kid looks up. Wonder fills his eyes. He pauses as if on the edge of saying something huge, but nothing much comes. Finally he stands and rounds the table with his hand outstretched. It's been a day, sir.

T. J. accepts his hand. Yes, it has. They shake.

Thank you.

The weight of the airman's grateful words hits T. J. like a bomb blast.

Rooster rejoins them at the kitchen window. Have we a Guardsman, Teej?

That we do, says T. J., softly, as a man who has already noticed the gray of tomorrow's sadness beginning to well inside.

The highly decorated U.S. Army Gunnery Sgt. Timothy James McVeigh waggles a thumb at the airman. This fine lad, a-lurkin', says he.

Well and good, calls Rooster. He reaches under his wing, pulls out a papyrus scroll, and opens it. Aye, says here, Guardsman, there is a young marine outside Falujah. A second baseman. A pure batsman and fleet of foot, it says. Early signs of shell shock, though. But there's a fine Major League baseball career awaiting him, if he can only make it home—as himself. He leaves the infirmary on the morrow. He heads for home in a couple of weeks. So, lad, in the next two weeks, you will be aiding and abetting this frazzled soul in living out a new dream he's about to have.

Which is?

Rooster hands him the scroll. With your help, it will soon occur to him to build a baseball field for the children of the town.

Baseball? In Iraq? The kid's head swivels between T. J. and Rooster, as if he's on the outside of an inside joke. How in the world would he—would we? . . .

T. J. throws an arm around him. What, don't you believe in baseball?

Well, yes. I do. Sure.

All right, then, says T. J. Go and do what you believe in.

AN INTERVIEW WITH THE ACTRESS CELESTE, OR, THE DREAMER AND THE DREAMED

{ SHARON DENNIS WYETH }

Sharon Dennis Wyeth charms us with a series of intriguing characters and unexpected plot twists. The story begins with an oracle and a prediction. Then follows blindness, an unexpected good marriage, poverty, an ugly evil dogcatcher, a capture, a kind canine, a mysterious girl rescuer, and, finally, the stage.

Tell us, dear lady, how did you come to be on the stage?

The answer to that question requires a story.

As a child, my mother was called to the cave of an oracle to help seal up a crack. The crack was not in the side of the cave, as you might think, but in the heel of the oracle's foot. It was said that the oracle, a fearsome shrouded creature, had been sitting at the cave's mouth since the beginning of time, so consumed with making predictions for the future that she never thought to change her position. Seated on the hard ground with her legs crossed, a bloody fissure had formed on her right heel. My mother's mother, who was known for herbal remedies, had concocted a salve that somehow made its way into the hands of a lady in the court of the emperor. Word got round of its healing properties, and one day my mother was dragged out of bed and ordered by a soldier to hand the salve over as it was needed to treat the oracle. For reasons of her own, my mother's mother refused to give the salve up unless her daughter was taken along to administer it.

"The salve alone is not a cure," my mother remembered her own mother saying to the soldier. "The touch of the person who applies the salve counts almost as much. If you really want to work a miracle on the oracle's foot, you'll take this child along."

A few weeks later, my terrified mother found herself seated on the ground of the musty cave, massaging the ancient creature's foot, which did not feel like flesh and blood to her but more like sandstone. The salve didn't actually heal the ulcer, she reported to me years later, but rather plugged it up, hardening enough to allow the oracle to sit with ease once more. In payment for the treatment she received, the oracle issued a prediction on my mother's behalf, an unheard-of honor for a poor peasant child.

"You shall dream a dreamer!" the oracle pronounced in a lazy sounding voice that seemed to bubble up from some deeper well-like place.

My mother, who was, after all, only a child at the time, hardly knew what to think. But there wasn't an extra moment to mull things over, since the oracle had another surprise in mind. After presenting my mother with the gift of a personal prediction, she took something away—my mother's sight. The explanation being that after rubbing the creature's foot, my mother, curious, as children tend to be, dared to take a peek at the oracle's face, something no other living person had dared do. Instead of killing her on the spot, the oracle showed some degree of compassion by blotting out the one offending sense, her sense of sight. Though she could not comprehend all this at first, my mother told me that in later years she came to view the incident not so much as the occasion for her punishment but an occasion on which she'd been spared. When she got back home, her mother wasted no time in bemoaning her daughter's condition. Instead she placed her energies into pushing the girl to develop in areas that would help make up for her lack of sight; chiefly her sense of touch, where she was already known to be gifted.

My mother's refined sense of touch led directly to a fortunate marriage to my father, a young stonecutter with a growing reputation. Both of them were on their hands and knees at the time. He was laying the floor in an outdoor courtyard; she was scrubbing the entryway of the palazzo next door. Being blind, she strayed a few inches or so to the area where he was working. Instead of scolding her, my father quietly observed the expression on her face. As her hands fell upon the newly laid marble, her face lit up with a radiant smile. "Exquisite," she murmured.

Hearing this, my father was quite pleased, of course.

But when my mother let her hand stray to the next tile over, her placid brow furrowed and her nostrils widened with disdain.

"What is it?" my father asked in alarm.

My mother cocked her head. "Crooked!"

"Impossible!" my father sputtered. "I'll prove it to you." He ran to fetch his level and laid it out on the spot. My mother was right, of course, her touch being supersensitive enough to pick up the tiniest degree of something not straight. My amazed father seized the opportunity and had her run her fingers over every inch of the newly laid floor, rechecking tiles with his level to make the minute corrections in the places she pointed out. When the project was done, the owners declared they had never seen a floor so flawless. Thus my father's reputation as a first-flight stonecutter was made and so was their marriage.

Though she was beneath his station, my father was smart enough to know that my mother's gift would greatly enhance his success. His decision to marry her was purely practical. Practical for them both, since, as a poor blind girl, she had long resigned herself to never having a husband or a home of her own. She felt herself so lucky in fact that she wondered whether her marriage to my father was part of the oracle's prediction.

"You shall dream a dreamer. . . ." That had been the creature's pronouncement. Yet her marriage to my father did not seem to fit. She had certainly not dreamed of a life as a stonecutter's wife. She hadn't dared to. In fact, she told me later that the only dream she ever had in her life was on the eve of my birth. She claims that she dreamed my face. . . .

I was born here in Erasone. My parents were not natives of the city. They moved here shortly before I was born. My father was sent here by the emperor himself to help in the final phase of construction of the theater. He covered the stage with marble; my mother was his assistant. I didn't know my father for very long. When I was eight years old he died from coughing blood. However, the eight short years I knew him were more than enough to imprint his character in my memory: though wielding the tools of his trade required brute strength, what distinguished him most was an unrelenting quest for perfection. I can only imagine Father's disappointment in having me as his child, for in those days I was diseased. I had a sort of sleeping illness that would come upon me no matter where I was or what I was doing. My father was utterly mystified by my behavior and I believe somewhat infuriated.

"Why is she sleeping now?" he would demand at the table, reaching across the table to rescue my three-year-old head from a bowl of porridge where it had fallen. "She's had a full night's rest."

My mother gently wiped my face with a warm cloth, while shaking my shoulder to wake me up. "I'm sure it has to do with the prophecy. It was said that I should dream a dreamer. What closer representation of a dreamer can you think of than one who sleeps in her porridge?"

However well my mother managed to explain away my oddity, it made me the object of ridicule when I was in public. In the city of Erasone I became a minor laughingstock known as "Simple" Celeste. I don't think that my father ever heard me called that. But I'm sure that my mother did with her keen sense of hearing, though she never brought it up.

As if the sleeping illness weren't enough, I had a second strange trait: at all costs I avoided the sight of my own reflection. If I spied a looking glass, I would run in the opposite direction; the same held true for bodies of water. I even made sure never to look too closely at the marble my father worked with once it was polished. I'm not sure what the explanation was for my behavior. It could have stemmed from my mother's blindness. A child's first mirror is, after all, her mother's eyes. As the mother gazes with love upon her child's face, the child sees herself as unspoiled perfection. This was out of the question for me, since my mother was blind. Perhaps the prospect of having a view of my face for the first time in an unloving looking glass was simply too frightening. The second explanation could have been that I assumed that I was ugly, having been branded as I was by the townspeople as "Simple Celeste." I do remember my mother once calling me beautiful. I was sitting on a stool next to the window while she dressed my hair. My hair was even thicker in those days and prone to tangling, but my mother's comb was patient.

"You are beautiful, Celeste," she pronounced.

"How can you tell, Mother, when you have never seen me?"

She stroked my forehead. "The day before you were born, I saw your face in a dream."

"Why do you believe in a dream?"

"It's the only dream I've ever had. If I don't believe in it, there will never be a dream in which I can believe. That would be sad, don't you think?"

"I suppose . . ." But I didn't believe her. There was no way she could know if I was beautiful without seeing me with her very own eyes.

When my father died, my mother was grief stricken. She had lost not only the love of her life but our way of life as well. Though my father's wages provided what was necessary for a good though modest life, there had never been enough to set aside. Nor was my mother welcome to work with other stone-cutters, her status having seemed to them somewhat out of order since she was neither an official stonecutter herself nor even a man. With my father's death, we were reduced to near poverty. My mother became a scrub maid again and I followed in her footsteps.

What hobbling figures we must have made setting off at dawn with rags to wipe the stoops of noble houses, erasing the signs of decadent midnight revels. We made them look respectable, my mother and I, and in return received tossed-out cuts of meat and crusts of day-old bread. At midday we would visit the theater. Some of the actors knew us and would let us in to sit at the very top with foreigners and the untouchables. What a bitter portion that was to swallow, the very theater that my father helped to build!—and in the farthest corner possible, there sat Mother and I, dressed in clothes almost as worn as the rags we used for our cleaning.

It was during this dark time that I met Peal the dogcatcher, a man with lips and tongue so thick his speech was impeded. His yellow eyes matched his yellow teeth. When I told Mother what he looked like, she guessed that Peal must not have been all human; have you ever seen a human with yellow eyes?

"Part wolf, I expect," said Mother. "Look out for him."

She was right to warn me, for from the moment we met, Peal made no secret of his attraction for me. For my part, never had there been anyone less attractive to me. In addition to his looks, there was his smell, a stew of rotted meat and onions, a combination I suppose of the food he fed to his charges before putting them to death and a fragrance he exuded due to his own diet. Mother sometimes detected Peal's presence a whole half day before he appeared—his odor preceded him so, along with the distant cries of the frightened canines imprisoned in the cart he dragged along with him. When he rounded the corner, I drew into myself trying to escape his notice. But his senses were as keen as Mother's where I was concerned. I felt his eyes boring into my back. "Good day, Mistress Celeste." His voice oozed.

"Get on your way," Mother chided. "Who are you to be addressing my girl?"

The churl dared to laugh. "I would not scoff at one who makes a decent wage, were I in your place. Poor blind woman, do you think your girl such a prize? Wedding me would only elevate her station. Look at her now!—her knees in the muck, dressed like a beggar. I even hear say she is marked with a disease where sleep overtakes her."

"She is the daughter of an artisan," Mother said in my defense. "And the habit she has of sleeping does not mark her as diseased but as one with a special destiny."

"Your mind is as cloudy as your vision," Peal mocked her.

I tossed my rag in his direction. "Don't you insult my mother!"

His wolflike eyes gleamed. "Very well then, Mistress Celeste, I'll leave off my suit for today."

Then he would shuffle on, dragging his caged cart behind him.

These visits left me cringing in shame and terror. If I were as beggarly as he described, would I not be forced in the end to accept a life with the dogcatcher? Mother was strong enough to work at the moment, but she would not always be. Nor would she always be with me. Father had made his departure to heaven without a jot of warning. Suppose the same were to happen with her? Would I be able to fare all alone in the world? The burden of these thoughts rendered my mind as bowed as my back, as day after day I knelt next to Mother, scrubbing and wondering what would come next.

I did not have to wait long for an answer. Mother grew sick and I had to work without her. "Keep awake!" she warned, as I left for the streets.

One morning she gave me a big stick. "If you feel yourself nodding, give yourself a tap on the head with this," she instructed.

I hid the stick in the folds of my skirt, fashioning a special pocket for it. As I made my way down the street, it nestled unseen next to my thigh. Wary of Peal and the danger he represented, I went over in my mind many times the manner in which I might protect myself, should he come upon me. In the scene I was invariably kneeling outside some palazzo or other; I smelled Peal approaching before I saw him. Pretending not to know he was coming, I would stealthily procure the heavy stick from the hidden pocket in my skirt and instead of hitting myself on the head, I'd strike him, swinging round with such unexpected force that the hulk would be thrown off his feet, his head hitting a cobblestone. As Fate would have it, quite a different scene occurred. During the time when Mother was still nursing her illness, I went out at dawn to clean the atrium of one Antonius, a man so rich he had commissioned a bust of himself in solid silver. Since I'd been working on my own for some weeks without incident, I'd let down my guard, taking in the brilliant light bouncing off the ornate buildings, allowing myself to gaze into a garden I was fond of passing because of its wonderful poppies. When arriving at the home of Antonius, I even allowed myself to rest back on my heels and take a nibble of the bread I'd brought to eat at midday. What happened next? I'm not certain; but at some point after the moment I rested back on my heels to take a nibble, my old sleeping sickness overtook me and I was captured by Peal.

The excruciating pain of being dragged by the hair woke me up. I screamed but my voice was soon drowned out by the howling of captive dogs. Without a word, monstrous Peal tossed me among them into the cart and dragged us all off to a kennel. He pitched me into the stinking cart right then and there with the dogs! I sat without shoes or scrub bucket, dumbfounded at my incompetence and terrified of being torn from limb to limb. As the kennel door sprang shut, I reached for the stick. Perhaps it wasn't too late to defend myself from the canines at least. But I needn't have bothered. Far from tearing me limb from limb, the dogs made room for me in their furry huddle, welcoming me as if I were kin. I fell asleep once more using one as a pillow.

What a disaster of a human being I was in those days, an almost orphan incapable of raising the tiniest defense against attack. Only through the kindness and mystery of nature am I alive today. The kindness refers to the animals in the pen where Peal kept me. I can't fathom why he did it, by the way. I had thought that he wished to have me as a wife. Perhaps he thought the dog kennel a safe place to keep me until he made the wedding arrangements. It could have been that he was afraid of Mother rising up from the sickbed. Blind as she was, Mother was far more capable and ferocious where my safety was concerned. It could be that Peal was waiting for Mother to die before bringing me out into the open and making our marriage official. In any event, Mother did not die then. Nor did she have to find me. My rescue came in the form of a girl with sparkling eyes. This girl is the mysterious part of nature that I mentioned. For I can only assume that she was a part of nature, fashioned out of the elements specifically for my rescue, since I only saw her that one time.

I had lost track of the number of days since my capture. I do know that I had made a new friend, the sable-haired creature I'd been using as a pillow. He licked my face every morning and shared his meat with me. This final thing is hard to imagine, I admit, but it did happen. When a sack of meat chunks and gristle happened to be tossed into the cage, the canines went mad, hurling themselves at the food and one another with teeth bared and claws lashing. Fear far outweighing hunger, I clung to the sides at these times, praying not to be mistaken for some bone or other. Fortunately, the chaos only lasted a moment or so, since that's how long it took for the food to be divided, each dog generally managing to get his teeth on some bit before retiring to gnaw. One day after one of these frenzies, the dog I used as a pillow sidled over with a chunk of meat hanging out of his mouth. Carefully biting off half, he let the extra piece fall into my lap. I stuffed it into my mouth without hesitating, heedless of its stench. From that day on, the creature shared with me. It is interesting to note here, that during the time of my captivity, I did not allow myself to rest. And by that I include the sleeping fits that had come upon me for years and left me vulnerable to Peal. I suppose I owe him that much. My captivity in the kennel frightened me out of my illness.

As for the girl who came to my rescue, she was a complete stranger, except that in some way she reminded me of how my mother might have looked when she was younger; only the girl wasn't blind. As I told you, her eyes sparkled. I trembled in fear for her, the day she came to the kennel. The dogs barked as she approached.

"Stay back!" I cried. "He will catch you! He will keep you prisoner as he keeps me prisoner!"

But she seemed not to hear me. Kneeling before the cage, she undid the latch, and remarkably the dogs grew quiet. One by one they ran out through the opening, except for my sable-haired friend, who kept by my side.

The girl beckoned to me. I crawled out of the kennel and picked up the dog, which seemed to weigh next to nothing. With the girl as my guide, I walked past a crooked hut where I suppose Peal might have brought me once we had been married. I felt my heart grow lighter as we continued along a sandstone path. The girl walked quickly, her long thick braid swinging down her back. We ran down some stairs cut into a hill. The sable-haired dog was still with me, tucked under my arm. The wind was perfectly still and quiet. I don't even remember the sound of a bird. At the bottom of the stairs there was a shallow body of water. I followed the girl and waded in, feeling the blood return to my ankles. She stopped for an instant and bent down to take a drink. I did the same and let the dog stand in the water beside me. Light bounced off the surface, searing my eyes. Next, we moved onto the bank. There were more stairs to climb, this time made of marble. Up above, I could see a platform of some sort with broken columns. The sky was a celestial blue. When we reached the platform, I looked out and saw the sea, stretching out before me. My nostrils took in a salty smell. The wind picked up and whipped around me. Tears of gratitude splashed my cheeks. I had never felt so free. I stepped a bit closer to my guide. I wanted to thank her for rescuing me and bringing me to such a beautiful place. But as I reached out to touch her shoulder, the girl with the sparkling eyes vanished. I was left standing in her place.

The sea became an ocean of faces and I was on the stage of this theater, my feet planted on the marble floor laid out by my father and mother. I stretched out my arms and bowed. The sable-haired dog that had stayed by my side barked and ran into the wings. I glanced out into the audience. There, reclining in a chaise, was the emperor himself, come all this way to see the performance!

Ever since that time, I have been here, as if this theater was the place I was born to be. So, the oracle's prediction came true, I suppose. For my mother's child is a dreamer. An actor must be a dreamer of sorts, giving shape to theatrical shadows. But make no mistake; I no longer sleep my life away. In this realm of dreams, I am fully awake.

MAJORITY RULES

{ NEAL SHUSTERMAN }

A boy climbs a mountain of challenging terrain to see what is on the other side. He wonders if the earth stops flat as some believe or if it goes beyond the mountain as others claim. A girl in a boat on a lake encounters a monster. But scientists say they have proof no monster exists. Reality and fantasy—which visions are true? Neal Shusterman mingles these alternatives, engaging the reader throughout the story.

"*What do you believe?*"

"*What I believe ain't any of your business.*"

"*Oh, but it is. It's more my business than you could possibly know.*"

"*I'm not talking to you about anything, I know my rights, I'm a minor, you can't keep me here. . . . What are you laughing at?*"

"*You think this is a police station? You think you're here because you shoplifted some music?*"

"Who says I did? You have no proof."

"Your petty thievery means nothing to me. That's not why you're here."

"Then what's this all about?"

"As I said, it's about what you believe. Forget about trying to defend yourself against an insignificant crime. I don't care what you stole, all I care about is the answer to my question. It's important that you tell me . . . what you believe."

"Why does it matter to you, what I believe?"

"When you were little, did you used to go to the playground?"

"What kind of stupid question is that?"

"Just answer it. Eventually you'll understand."

"Yes, I went to a playground when I was a kid. So what?"

"Did you ever go on a seesaw?"

"Of course. Does all this have a point?"

"Tell me what makes a seesaw work."

"You sit on one side, somebody sits on the other, you go up and down. Are we done yet?"

"Did you ever sit on the other side from one of your parents?"

"Yeah."

"What happened?"

"It doesn't work, they're too heavy. You stay up in the air."

"Ah, so the balance shifted entirely to the other side."

"I still don't get what this has to do with me."

It is the year 1375, by the Julian calendar. The boy climbs a mountain. He knows he's not supposed to, he's been told never to climb the mountain. No one who has ever climbed the mountain has returned, and for good reason. These mountains, these jagged stone teeth thrust up through the earth, are a barrier. A barrier made by God to keep humble human beings from seeing what lies on the other side. All his life, the boy has wanted to climb the mountain, and now at thirteen he's finally gotten up the nerve. Only halfway up, his sandals are worn and his bones ache, but a driving will to know pushes him forward. If it is true that this is indeed the edge of the earth, it will be spectacular. Not just the view but the knowledge of the truth will be spectacular, for then it will be more than just belief—more than mere tales told by grandparents. The power of knowing that this truly is the edge, and that nothing lies beyond it but the emptiness of space, will be the greatest power the boy could know. "I have been there," he could tell his friends, and someday his children. Although they may not believe him, he will know the truth of it.

The old people all say that the earth is a flat disc. He wants to believe this, because there's comfort in knowing that the old ones are right. But not everyone thinks as the old ones do. There is talk of an ancient mathematician whose work proved otherwise. Dangerous people now spout heresy left and right, claiming that the world is round, and say that they have mathematical evidence to prove it. More and more people are coming to believe this, accepting the mathematician's version of things as the truth.

The boy doesn't know what to believe, so he has to see for himself. He has to know.

His sandals are torn to shreds by the time he nears the peak of the mountain. Hand over hand he climbs, it seems only a few feet to the top, but every few feet yields more rock above him. His fingers are worn to the bone but he will not stop—

and at last, after hours, after days, he finally crests the top and looks into the distance to see the most awe-inspiring sight of his young life:

Nothing.

He sees nothing beyond the mountain.

The earth stops here. Above the sky is still blue, but beyond the edge it fades into a darkness filled with stars that stretch to infinity. So it's true, then! This is the edge, and the world is flat!

But then a wind blows up from the face of the mountain, kicking dust into his eyes. He turns away, he closes his eyes. All at once he feels a change—a change in balance, a change in equilibrium—as if someone far away has reached out and pulled a rug out from underneath him. He clings to the mountain to keep from falling, and he blinks to clear the dust from his eyes. When he looks out again over the edge, the sight is not quite so marvelous anymore. Suddenly before him where a moment ago there was star-filled space are sunlit hills leading down into a green valley, and beyond the valley more mountains. The earth doesn't stop here. It goes on, and on, and on.

He cannot explain it. He cannot understand what has happened between one moment and the next. Now his vision of the flat earth is suddenly gone. *Perhaps*, he thinks, confused to the very core of his being, *perhaps it was just my imagination, and perhaps the world is round after all.*

"What if everything is like that seesaw? What if everything we know as reality is as unstable as the shifting of a seesaw?"

"I think you're crazy and I want to get out of here."

"In time, but first you must make a decision."

"If this isn't a police station, then what is it? If I haven't been arrested then why am I here?"

"Fear won't help you now. You need a clear mind. Your decision must come from a clear mind."

"A decision about what?"

"About what you believe."

"I believe lots of things."

"Do you believe in God?"

"Yes."

"Do you believe that the universe is infinite?"

"Yes."

"Do you believe there is life on other worlds?"

"Uh, yeah, I guess."

"And do you believe that life on other worlds is friendly or hostile?"

"I don't know."

"Ah! Well, I think we've finally discovered why you're here."

The girl is tired of TV, and so she decides to go out in a boat. It's her favorite thing to do. She would usually take a boat out as far as she could on the cold, deep lake, then lean back with a book, and read until the sun sank low in the sky. But today there's something strange in the air—an eerie sense of foreboding she can feel even before she pushes the rowboat from shore. She's about three hundred yards out when she feels the boat rock.

A school of fish, she thinks, *perhaps a turtle*. Sure, that's all it is. The loch is full of many large creatures and most are harmless.

Yes, many large creatures and one immense one, if you believe the legends.

The girl doesn't know whether she believes them, but she would tell stories to the tourists just as everyone did, because tourists are her family's bread and butter, and who would come to the loch at all, if it weren't for the legends of Nessie?

She's reaching down for her book and so she doesn't see it at first. All she sees is a shadow cast over the pages, and when she looks up, there it is blocking out the sky: a massive head, gravestone gray and dripping with slime. Its eyes are way too small and it bares a gaping maw of teeth. She draws in a breath, but so terrified is she that her throat closes and she can't scream. All she can do is look at that awful tooth-filled mouth moving down towards her, ready to swallow her whole. And then suddenly just before it reaches her, there comes a twinkling of light, and the entire thing dissolves into shimmering dust. Not just its head but its body beneath the water vanishes so suddenly the water rushes in to fill the empty space, almost sinking her boat.

And when the rushing water settles, there she is in a half-flooded boat, three hundred yards off the shore of Loch Ness. Trying not to think about what has just happened, she rows back to shore in a daze, her body numb from the icy water that has inundated her boat. She steps through the front door of her family's cottage, trying to figure out how to tell her parents what she had just seen, but finds that she can't tell them.

Her father turns to her. "You missed the show," he says. "There were these lousy scientists, said they proved beyond a shadow of a doubt that Nessie don't exist. They made a sonar sweep of the whole loch, they did. A sonar sweep!"

"Mmm," says her mother, shaking her head. "I dare say millions of people must'a tuned in to watch."

"And all around the world, too," adds her father. "They've been showing the blasted thing for days."

Her mother sighs. "That's going to hurt the tourist trade. All those people no longer believing in Nessie . . ."

"The aliens—are they hostile or are they friendly? Quickly, there's not much time."

"I'm not telling you anything until you tell me who you are, and why it's so important."

"Very well, then . . . I've been called many things, throughout history . . . but based on the current majority belief system, I am what you would call . . . an angel."

"An angel . . ."

"Don't look so shocked, it's nothing too spectacular, really. I'm just a servant of the universe, same as you. A servant performing a function."

"I never really believed in angels. . . ."

"It doesn't matter if you believe in angels; what matters is that enough people do believe in them to make me one."

"I don't understand."

"Reality is a fluid thing, always changing. What was true a thousand years ago is not true now. For instance, a thousand years ago the majority of people believed the world was flat and so it truly was flat, but there came a moment in time when there was a perfect balance. A moment in time when exactly half of humanity believed that it was flat . . . and half believed that it was round. It is my job to come to the world in that moment of balance."

"And do what?"

"And locate the person who will shift the balance to one side or the

other. Like a seesaw. You see, when it comes to what is real and what is not, majority rules."

"And what does that have to do with me?"

"In just a few minutes your world is going to change forever, and you, my friend, are the fulcrum."

"Fulcrum?"

"The pivot point on which everything rests. Everyone else in the world has already confirmed their belief as to whether or not life in the greater universe is hostile or friendly. Even if they haven't voiced their opinion aloud, they've come to a decision in their own mind. But you are still uncertain. You stand right in the balance, halfway between one future and another. What you believe will cause the seesaw of reality to shift to the left . . . or to the right."

"What I believe?"

"Yes, exactly. What . . . you . . . believe . . ."

"It's not fair! How can everything rest on me?"

"You've spent your youth stealing trinkets without taking responsibility. Now responsibility has come calling upon you. I would say that's more than fair. It's justice."

"I know what I want to believe."

"What you want to believe, and what you truly believe aren't always the same thing. . . . Reach down. Discover where your belief lies. I know you enjoy playing games of world annihilation at the hands of ruthless, heartless beings. Now it's time to find out if you see those dark visions as true, or are they, after all, just games."

"I need more time!"

"There is no time! By my calculations you have less than one minute left. The decision must be made by then, and I cannot make it for you, so think! In your heart of hearts, are they are hostile . . . or friendly? . . ."

In another part of the world, a young boy stands in his family's rye field while his father tries to make sense of what he sees. The whole family is there, father, mother, sister. Not necessarily because they *should* be there but because in times of confusion and fear it simply seems best for them to stay together. The crop circles have appeared overnight for three nights in a row. It is clear by their size and their symmetry that this is not a joke put on by other kids in the small town. There is no one in town smart enough to pull this off and get away with it. People scoffed—accused the family of doing it themselves. People looked suspiciously at the boy, and at his parents and sister. That is, until they came to their field and saw the formations themselves ... and smelled the strange odor in the air. It isn't a stench, just an aroma; organic, yet completely unknown. It's the musk of some creature, that human senses instinctively know is not of this world.

"Look! Over there!" At the sound of his sister's voice, they all turn to the north and a vision assaults the boy's eyes, filling him with absolute terror.

Impossible crafts of unimaginable size loom over the hillside fields, getting closer. They have no wings, yet they hover in the air. Suddenly weapons fire, tearing holes into the hills themselves. Silos, barns and neighboring farmhouses explode in balls of flame.

The boy runs to his father, clinging to him. His mom screams, and picks up his sister, who buries her face against Mom's blouse.

"Daddy, do something!" the boy says, but even as he says it, he knows there is nothing his father can do. All he can do is hold his son with his strong hands, and watch. The boy will not watch this horror. Instead he closes his eyes waiting for the end, but the end doesn't come. . . .

. . . and as he waits, something changes. . . .

He can sense the change around him, subtle and strange, like a static charge in the air. Instinctively he knows that something has shifted like a seesaw tilting from left to right. He opens his eyes. The ships are still there, but there are no weapons firing, no hills on fire, and the barns, farmhouses, and silos are untouched. Not a single one has been damaged. *Was it my imagination?* he thinks. *It must have been.*

As he holds his father tight, the first ship in the armada lands right before them. A hatch opens, spilling forth light. The family cannot see through the blinding light of the doorway, but they can hear a voice, solemn, and serene.

"We are here to welcome your world into the larger community," the voice says, with a deep sense of soothing assurance.

"We come as friends."

THE HIDDEN GIRL

{ TAMORA PIERCE }

An itinerant priest travels the countryside with his daughter, Teky, daring to teach from forbidden books—a perilous undertaking. If discovered by temple priests, they face death. For they live in a land where women are deprived of rights. They may not be taught reading and writing. When her father dies, Teky must find a way to continue her mission—even at the risk of her own life....

It was late in the summer when my father brought me to the house of my aunt and uncle in the town of Hartunjur. I was relieved to be with them, because my aunt was my father's older sister. When she heard his deep, racking cough, she summoned a healer and ordered my father to submit to his care. I had begged him to do so for weeks, but a daughter's word did not have the weight of an older sister's, even if that daughter did his reading to make up for his fading vision.

That evening, as the healer examined my father, the innkeeper next door gave two strangers permission to sleep in his loft. Helping my aunt and cousins to prepare our supper, I learned the young man, Fadal, was handsome if beardless, and quite funny. His companion, Qiom, was very tall and dark, with an odd, slow way of speaking.

"As if," said my aunt, "he had only recently learned to talk."

I told this to my father as I brought his supper to him. Father shook his head. "Have you women nothing more to do than gossip about men?" he asked.

He looked weary and sad. I answered in the voice I had perfected for his amusement, that of my grandmother, Omi Heza. "Why should we not, whippersnapper?" I asked, surprising a smile from him. "In the Book of the Distaff it says that a woman's greatest weapon is her reason, and her greatest shield is her knowledge. . . ."

Father shook his head. "The temple priests are in the right of it after all, and the first error lies in teaching women to read," he said, his eyes twinkling. "And your mother and I made our second error when we let you stay with my mother when you were young! If I did not look at you, I would swear she was here to scold me."

I grinned at him. He did so like it when I made Omi Heza live again, even briefly.

That night I had the strangest dream. A voice that was two voices, a man's and a woman's, speaking as one, called to me. "Look. What lies before you?"

Before me stood veiled women, dressed in strict black from head to feet, some even covered in black to the roots of their fingers and toes. Their eyes watched me from the windows of their veils, brown, gray-green, blue-gray, all the colors of my people, set in every shade of brown and bronze skin, firmly young to dry with age.

"I see women and girls," I replied at last. Somehow I knew the voice was that of the God in the Flame, who spoke to my own Oracle. "I see watchfulness and waiting. I see silence."

"What else do you see?" asked the God's intertwined voices.

"I see veils."

"Then you do not see everything."

With that I woke. Since it was dawn, I chose to prepare myself for the day. Once I had put on my veils, I picked up the yoke with the buckets and went to fetch water for my aunt. I passed few other people. Most women preferred to wait until later in the day to fill the water jars for their houses. On my fourth trip, one other person was at the well filling buckets, the young man Fadal whom my cousins had talked about.

I did nothing so improper as acknowledge him. One of my cousins might smooth a sleeve or look at him sidelong. They were more daring than I. They also had prettier eyes and longer lashes. I bent to my work.

"How do you stand it?" To my shock, the voice was Fadal's. "Doing all that draped in veils? A slave in chains has more freedom to move."

Without moving my head, I looked around. We were quite alone. People were inside, eating breakfast. Worse—or better, I wasn't sure which—this Fadal spoke with the barest move-ment of his mouth in a soft, carrying tone. Girls learned it young. Had he imitated his mother and aunts, before they told him men never had to talk that way?

"Don't you want to throw the whole bundle in the priests' faces? Tell *them* to wear veils, if they like them so much?"

Some of the things he said were complaints I had made, it's true. Every girl has. Every girl who is not a twittering pushover for the nearest creature to grow a mustache. But still . . .

"Said like a man," I replied in that secretive way, only better, because I was more practiced. "You see only the outsides of things, when it is we women who see the heart of it all." I checked our surroundings a second time before I went on. "These veils are freedom, beardless *boy*. Before I put them on, I was a sheep on the market. My nose was longer than my cousin's, my skin not so fine as my mother's, my hair not so curly as my aunt's. My teeth, my weight, my length of bone— pick, pick, pick. Then I put on the veil. Poof! The gossips have only my eyes, my hands, my voice, my feet. They must judge me on my value to my family, and my family values me for who I am and what I can do."

"You *like* the veil?" He seemed so shocked! "You like being hidden away?"

"I *like* keeping myself to myself. My heart is hidden. It is mine," I told him. "And . . ." Suddenly I remembered the dream, the many women in black. "If you wished to have me beaten for speaking to a man, how would you find me? I could vanish among a crowd of women, and you would never even know which of us you spoke to."

"But you have no power," he protested. Now he sounded weak, or thoughtful, perhaps both.

"Again, said like a man who wears his thoughts on his face."
Really, I was getting tired of this pup. "No power? Who cooks
for you, when you have a home? Who weaves and sews the
clothes you wear, the sheets and blankets you sleep in? Who is
awake while you sleep? No power? Ask yourself how much
power a woman has, the next time she hands you a bowl of
food. And taste it carefully."

My buckets were full. I shouldered my yoke, silently cursing
as my veil twisted and caught under it, and walked away, careful not to spill any water. I was almost to my aunt's house when
I heard shouting. I looked back. Some of the village boys had
come to pick a fight with Fadal, who knew over what. Boys
were always fighting, particularly with strangers. I went into
my aunt's house and closed the door behind me.

I had just finished topping off the water jars when the
innkeeper's wife came and pulled my aunt out into the courtyard. They whispered together urgently for a moment. Then
my aunt ordered us girls to get into the kitchen and stay there.
Swiftly she closed the kitchen doors and shutters before she
went back to the courtyard and her friend. My cousins and I
listened at the cracks in the shutters and doors, hearing distant
male shouts. The noise faded, leaving us no wiser than before.

I finally gave up. My father needed his breakfast. We would
hear the news soon enough. "What is going on?" he asked as I
brought his simple meal. He was dressed already. From the
smell of medicinal herbs, the healer had visited him while I
was away.

"They did not tell us. We are only silly young girls," I
grumbled.

"And how do they expect you to learn wisdom?" my father

asked me as I guided his hand to his plate and cup. "Read to me, my treasure? From the Book of the Distaff, the third chapter, the fifth lesson."

I had reached the verse concerning balance in the land and water when my uncle and aunt interrupted us. "Quickly, quickly," my uncle said. "Teky, come with us. The girls must go into the hidden room. The temple priests have found a woman dressed as a man—that boy Fadal, who stayed at the inn last night. They are taking her to the temple for burning. They will come for our girls next, to see if they were contaminated by the nearness of this Fadal."

I stayed where I was. I knew my father. He turned his fading eyes on his brother-in-law. "Is the faith of your girls so weak, that your temple priest will break it?" he asked gently. "Or is your priest so stupid, that he will find failure where there is none?"

My aunt folded her hands and unpinned her face veil. "That is what I told you," she said to her husband. "We have raised our girls to follow the Oracle's laws. They are no shame to us, that we must hide them."

"We could be accused of impurity!" whispered my uncle. His face was covered in greasy sweat. "We live next door to the inn, they may think we are tainted!"

My father shook his head. "Purity of faith is yours alone, brother. Only you can speak for it, and the only one to whom you should ever speak of it is the God. Not to a priest who teaches you only from half of the Oracle's books."

"And *that* is the kind of talk that will get my daughters burned if they repeat it!" my uncle cried. "We are sheltering heretics!"

My father looked down. "If you are no longer happy to house my daughter and me, then we shall find another roof, or the God's own stars," he said. "We will not disturb the peace of this house, brother. But do you really wish to live in fear of those who claim to speak for the God who cooks our food, heats our homes, lights our lamps? The God in the Flame shines in the eyes of your wife and daughters, and in the sky by day and night. That god speaks with two voices, male and female, has two faces, the sun and the moon, and spoke through an Oracle who wrote two books, not one. Nothing changes that."

My uncle turned on his heel and walked out. My aunt followed him. Once they were gone, my cousins crept in, their eyes wide in fear. To soothe them, my father had me continue to read from the forbidden half of the Oracle's texts, the Book of the Distaff. I stopped reading on my aunt's return.

"He went to the temple, to witness Fadal's burning. He fears what they would say if he was not there, but he did not say to send the girls to the hidden room," she said, sinking down onto a pillow. "He hears what you say, brother, but he has lived in this town all his life. The temple priesthood is strong here. Until you came, the wandering priesthood was represented only by your letters and our own readings of the forbidden texts."

"Should we go to the hidden room now?" asked my oldest cousin, her voice trembling. "I hate it, but if they come testing . . ."

"They would not dare, my treasure," my aunt said. "They must not dare. Surely even they know that to burn the children of respectable citizens . . . There are reasons it has not been done for so long."

"A girl," my youngest cousin said, amazed. "A girl, dressing as a man. Why would anyone want to do that?"

"What of his companion?" asked my father. "The strange fellow, Qiom, did I hear his name was? Has anyone told him?"

"If he is wise, he has fled. Otherwise they will burn *him*," said my aunt.

Since it was time to cook lunch, my father went to sit in the kitchen with us. My uncle found us there. He was ashen, as if he had seen his world unmade.

"It was the other one, the stranger Qiom," my uncle said as he sat at the kitchen table. "He ripped the doors from the temple. He beat every man who tried to lay hands on him. He killed the priest by throwing him into the wall. Then he took Fadal, and he ran from the town before they could close the gates." He mopped his face with the wet cloth my aunt brought for him. "No man can run so fast! No man could have ripped the temple doors from their hinges! It is a sign from the God in the Flame! A sign, that he sent this creature to save this woman!"

"But the God has never spoken in such a fashion before," said my father gently. "Brother, compose yourself. Breathe with the quiet strength of your wife and daughters. See how they wait? They do not spend themselves in panic."

My cousins and I rolled our eyes and my aunt smiled. My father's idea of womanhood was idealized. He always forgot that my mother was not above screaming if she saw a furred spider or panicking if a temple priest looked at her the wrong way.

Sometime after lunch the greatest piece of news came, brought by other men who shared readings in the forbidden texts with my uncle and aunt. The temple had burned down. Somehow wood had fallen into its great fire as Qiom rescued Fadal, setting the place ablaze. Now many of the people of Hartunjur asked each other if the God whose sole text was the Book of the Sword would have let his temple be destroyed by a creature who came to save a woman who had dressed as a man. Hearing that a wandering priest who taught the forbidden texts was in the town, they came to hear what the temple priests had not taught them.

My father talked to the men about what the temple priests left out of the Oracle's writings. He taught them about the Oracle's wise wife, who was his first councillor. He told my favorite story, one almost forgotten in the lands where the God in the Flame and the Oracle were supreme, of the Oracle's oldest daughter, the general who had dressed in armor to defend her father's temple city.

At last my father's cough returned ferociously. As the healer brought him a cup of syrup, my father waved to me. "Teky, read to them," he said, his voice hoarse. "Read to them from the Book of the Distaff." He raised his voice to the men. "This is not in your copies of the Oracle's Books," he said, and coughed for long moments. He swallowed a mouthful of syrup, then continued, "It is this the temple priests do not want you to hear. Tekalimy will read to you."

"A woman!" someone in the back of the room cried. "Reading!"

My father half rose from his cushions. "Have you heard

nothing of what I have said?" he demanded. His cheeks were flushed with his rising fever. I reached out to calm him, to press him back down to his cushions, but he shook off my hand. "Without our women we are only half of ourselves! If our women are unclean, we are half unclean! Teky! Read!"

I stood, trembling, the book open and heavy in my hands. Never had I read before so many men. Never had I seen so many angry pairs of eyes, all burning me where I stood. Who was I? Would someone here betray me when the Council of Priests sent a new man here?

Then I remembered my words just that morning to Fadal. Under the black veil that covered my mouth, I smiled. Who could identify me? I was another set of black veils among a town full of them. Once I was away from my father, I was simply another pair of eyes, another pair of feet.

As for those men's eyes burning me, they touched only my veils. I was safe inside them, looking out. They could no more know what was in my heart than they could know my face.

I began to read the Oracle's words. "If you look at the God and see only the sun, you see only half the God," I read. My voice shook, then steadied. I had been reading these words all my life. "If you look at humanity and see only man, you see only half of your soul. Attend to women as you attend to men, with heart and mind intent." From the corner of my eye I could see my father nod as, coughing softly, he drank the rest of his medicine.

I read until he raised his hand, then closed the book. As he leaned forward to question the men on what they had heard, I retired with the book in my hands, as I often did. I went no farther than my aunt's kitchen. She was the only one there. "Come," she said, and took me to a stable down the street. There I found women and girls, the families of the men who talked now with my father. They too had come for learning, summoned by my aunt and cousins, who had prepared them for me. They too were shaken by the events in the temple. While I had read to the men, they had listened in the shadows and outside the windows. Now my aunt and my cousins gave out slates and chalk, or worn copies of The Book of the Sword: the Lessons of the Law.

"The Book of the Sword?" asked one newcomer, frightened. "Are you mad? It is forbidden to us!"

I opened the Book to the Lesson of Family and read, "Only by reading will the word of the God in the Flame blaze clearly in the eyes of all. If your wife does not read, you must teach her. It is your sacred duty, and the sacred duty of your wife, to teach your children to read. Without reading, we are all without light in the dark, without fire in the cold." I closed the Book and said to the newcomer, "This is the beginning to the most important lesson in the Book of the Sword: the Lesson of the Rights of Women under the Law of the God. How many of you can read?"

They raised their hands. My aunt and cousins had been busy: half of them could read. Now, without my telling them, those who could moved to share books with those who could not as I read the first lesson for all to hear. From the letters that made it up, the others would begin to learn to read, but they would also hear their rights as set out by the Oracle. Even temple priests would have to acknowledge them if these women petitioned the courts for their rights under the Book of the Sword.

"If a woman shall bear a man's children and he divorces her, he is forbidden to turn her out of his house penniless. If he does so, she may appeal to the court of the temple," I read. I heard chalk squeak as the women wrote that down. "All men know this. The God did not wish us to be without power. The God did not tell the Oracle to make us powerless," I explained. Father did not know I used the Lesson of the Law. I was only supposed to teach them to read. But he had never said what I was to use, and he could hardly quarrel with how I taught when he was not there to hear me.

I did not say more than that, however. I had to be careful. I had to let them think about the words, and I had to leave time for them to concentrate on forming the letters. And I could not press them too hard. Four years ago a woman had complained to her husband that I was trying to turn the women against the men. That was when my mother was still alive. She was too shy to teach, but she had whipped me over the woman's complaint.

"Our lives are on the razor's edge!" she had scolded me after the beating. "Because you are clever, because you are the pearl of his eye, your father trusted you, but you go too far! You cannot bully people into change, Teky! We are like our land, with the very stones to serve us for veils. Rain change on us too much, too fast, and we do not drink it up. We flood, destroying everything in our way. Your lectures will bring death on us, on your father and me, and on you. Now. Will you teach them to read, just read, or will I tell your father you cannot be trusted with our lives?"

But don't you *see*? I had wanted to ask her then, and I still asked her ghost. Don't you see that the women need to know what is there? That the Book of the Sword already holds rights that the temple priests have to respect? I could *show* the women how to do it.

But I bowed to my mother, and told myself I would just take more time. I would make the women see how to do it, that was all. Not push them. Not lecture them. Only read to them what was in the book, and trust them to think about it, as my father trusted me to teach them to read. As even my mother trusted me to teach them again, after a while. As she trusted me to look after my father.

I crouched to help a girl perfect her writing of the word *law*. My problem was that I wanted to help them *all*, my father, the women, and the girls. They would have laughed at me, had they known. One sixteen-year-old girl, not even married, they would say. You can't even look after yourself!

Fadal would say that. Fadal, who thought my veils were chains. Poor Fadal, whose only way to deal with being a woman was to try to be something she was not.

As the shock of the temple's destruction grew in the town, the attendance at my father's lessons grew every day, and so did the attendance at mine. A week passed, then two. We had never stayed so long in one place. It worried and pleased me. A longer stay meant the chances were greater that those who ruled the temple priests in distant Kenibupur stood a better chance of hearing of our activities. At the same time, the healer was able to banish most of that cough from my father's chest, which was all to the good. For once I saw the girls who started their first letters under my eye master their first short sentences. We could celebrate my oldest cousin's betrothal. I even dreamed of attending her wedding, but that was not to be. As the winds began to scour the mountain passes, word came that new temple priests were coming to serve the town again. My father took it as a sign to be on our way.

We left better provided for than we had been in years, three weeks after the day I talked to Fadal. Our donkey's packs were heavy, and I carried my share of the weight, too. One of the men who had studied with us sent us to his family's village, where we would be welcome. He told us as well of caves along the road where we could shelter at night. The routine was like settling into a shabby, familiar pair of sandals.

I built a fire at the mouth of the cave that first night. Once it was going, my father helped me to cook supper, and he cleaned our dishes in the nearby stream. Afterward we sat in silence, watching the flames. Finally I asked him what I had so often asked as a child, "Do you see the God in the Flame?"

He sounded amused when he said, "I see the God in your bright eyes, Teky." After a while he sighed, and remarked, "It is strange, to be traveling again, is it not?"

I nodded. "My aunt's home is a good place to live."

"I have been thinking. If something happens to me . . ."

I started to protest. Father held up his hand, his old signal for me to be silent. I hated it when he talked that way, he knew I hated it.

"If something happens to me, return to your aunt's house. She will arrange a good match for you, every bit as good as the one she arranged for your cousin." My father nodded as if he agreed with himself. "We talked about it. She knows what to do."

"Now, see here, my boy," I began in Omi Heza's old voice, thinking to joke him out of his decision.

He raised a hand. "Hush, Teky. This is no laughing matter." He took up the Book of the Distaff and began to read.

I continued to watch the fire, but instead of warmth, a creeping veil of cold eased up my back, my shoulders, and over my head and face. Go to my aunt's house, and wait to be married? When all I had done for the last five years of my life was this? Walk the roads of our country, talk to women and girls, men and boys, hear their stories, cook and eat with them, visit their homes, sew and weave with them, feed their babies and hold the hands of their grandfathers and grandmothers? I had cobbled sandals, made round bread, gathered honey, milked cows and goats and sheep and even mares. In one village I had twisted rope, in others I helped to bring animals in from dust and sandstorms. In the mountains in the spring I had waded up to my waist in floodwater to save a child who had strayed. In stick huts in forests I had brewed medicines. In three cities I sold fruit and honey in the marketplace. In a hundred marketplaces, big and small, I had studied with my parents and learned to dicker with merchants on my own. In my short sixteen years I had eaten hummus made at least thirty different ways. Sitting by this small fire with my back to a hollow in a hill, I could feel my world shrink to the size of a sun-dried brick house, of a village wall. To know only the same faces for the rest of my life, with only a light seasoning of new ones . . .

I think I slept where I sat, because the flames parted at their bases, opening like a blossom to reveal orange coals that rippled with heat and bits of blue fire. Dreaming, I knew the God had come.

"Did you hear?" I asked the God as if he, she were one of my cousins who had been sitting close by. "He just . . . he decided. He didn't ask me, he just decided. Why didn't he even tell me what he was thinking?"

"He is a man," said both halves of the God, woman and man. "He has never been stripped of his voice, so he does not know how it feels to be stripped of it, even a little. Now I, I understand it very well. I have been stripped of half my voice for centuries of your time. My man voice thunders clearly— wrongly, sometimes, thanks to the priests who decided what words of my Oracle they would repeat, but clearly. But no one hears my woman voice anymore. I would like my woman voice back. You would like *your* voice back. And this man who loves you will never realize it. Don't you ever wonder who *will* realize it, Tekalimy?"

"Teky, Teky." My father was shaking my shoulder. "You are sleeping where you sit. Go to bed. I will bank the fire."

I looked up at him, blinking, my eyes hot and dry. They felt as if I had never closed them. "What if I do not want to go to my aunt and have a husband, Father?" I asked, my voice very tiny.

"Don't be silly," he said, kissing my cheek. "What else would you do? Go to bed."

I looked at the fire. If the flames had parted, they were joined again now.

As I unrolled my blankets and covered myself up, I admitted he had made a good point. What else would I do?

The next village already knew of the destruction of the Hartunjur temple. As soon as the priest finished each night's lesson and banked the fire, many of the men who heard him came to the man who housed my father and me, to hear my father teach, to hear me read, and to talk with my father about what the reading meant. That first night, as I always did in a strange town, I went to our host's wife. I found her in her kitchen, having tea with friends. Hurriedly they fastened their veils. Among strangers, even women, we all kept our veils on during these meetings. We needed only one weak or frightened soul to report our true names and faces to the priests for there to be a burning that would be remembered for centuries.

"Excuse me," I said politely, keeping my eyes down, "but I know it is hard to hear at the windows and doors. There is no reason why your thirst should go unslaked while men talk. Would you like for me to read more of the Books to you?"

Someone gasped. They all drew back as if I were a viper.

"How did you know we listened?" my hostess demanded. She trembled all over.

I passed my hand across the veil over my mouth, the sign that showed I was smiling. "We survive in a man's world by learning all we can," I reminded them, just as I had reminded my father in my grandmother's voice. This was an old, old ritual for me. I followed it in every new village. "Knowledge keeps us ahead of them and better able to guide them, is it not true, my sisters? Will you not drink more from the Oracle's well of knowledge?" I asked, and raised the Books in my hand.

And so we fell back into our routine, which was the same, but changed. The story of Qiom and Fadal had raced ahead of us. It was autumn, then winter, but people traveled, just as my father and I traveled. The temple priests were more suspicious of newcomers as the story grew in its spreading. We no longer dared stay for more than a few days in each village, though those who came to hear us grew in numbers. For my father, the change was noticeable, though not startling. But for me . . .

For every three new men who came to hear my father, I met five new women and girls. In some villages, it might be seven and eight more women than I might have seen before. In December we stayed in a town for ten days, the longest stay since Hartunjur. I remembered it not only because a man and five boys came to hear *me*, leaving my father's lesson when I did, but because it was here that my father's cough returned.

We left the town because a delegation from the temple court at Kenibupur was expected to arrive within days, to honor the town by celebrating the Longest Night festival there. We dared not stay with so many temple priests on their way. Instead, despite my father's worsening health, we took the road to the next village. I had thought the boys in that place would be different. They would not be so bored, or so used to following their mothers, as to be curious about my lessons. I was wrong. Two grown men from that tiny village joined three boys to hear my teaching on the Oracle's law concerning their wives and daughters.

We traveled on three days later, with the priest practically snuffling at our host's door. My father's voice was ragged and cracked from coughing, despite the good healer who had attended him there. Putting her herbs and medicines away, she had shaken her head at my father. When he glanced over to see if I had noticed, I pretended to do something else. He *must* get well, I told the God. Who will teach them if he dies?

That night I heard the God's voices again, and saw the field of veiled women. "What do you see?" asked the God.

"People who can do nothing for my father," I said in bitterness, and turned my back on them.

"Then you are blind," said the God.

Two villages later, I was teaching the women, all of their children, and an old man about a daughter's right of inheritance when a boy came to fetch me. My father had lost his voice as he was teaching. "You will answer the questions for me, Teky," he whispered in my ear.

"I think you should stop!" I whispered back, frightened. His chest clattered softly like dried leaves stirred by the wind. "You are ill, you should rest."

"When will another of us wandering priests come?" he whispered. "You will tell them my answers *now*."

"Why do the temple priests keep the Book of the Distaff from us?" a man wanted to know when my father made a sign for another question. "Why risk offending the God in the Flame and the Oracle's spirit?"

"Because people who are ignorant are more easily led," I replied, making my voice as strong as I could. They could not see me waver. "The God has not punished the priests, so they believe the God will *never* punish them. And they know that fear makes people easily led. If they teach you that your women are devilish forces, mysterious and not to be trusted, you will fear them. You will turn to your priests to protect you from these veiled creatures."

"Is that your father who speaks?" an old man demanded angrily. "Or is it you, taking advantage of a sick man?"

My father raised his hands. He pointed to himself.

"My father says that the words are his. *I* tell you that I have heard this answer many dozens of times," I replied as the other men chuckled. "Many men have asked it."

I had to give my lesson in reading and the law during the noon hour the next day. My father's voice came back for a short time the next night, then failed. Once again he needed me to speak for him. The same was true of the third night.

The God came back, and showed me the veiled women. "Wake up, Teky!" she said, he said, as one. "There are your sisters, your mothers, your aunts, your cousins. What do you see?"

"People I can barely snatch the time to teach!" I cried. "People who have rights under the Book of the Sword that is on the altar of every temple! People who don't have to show the priests a book they will get burned for possessing if they want justice!"

"So this is progress," the God told me. "But you have yet to give the simplest answer of all. It is truly there, in what you told Fadal, Teky. Only speak the answer that matters, and I will take you into my service. You will become my new Oracle, the one to speak my truth completely."

"I don't want to be an Oracle," I muttered. "I just want to teach my sisters their rights under the law."

A hand on my shoulder joggled me awake. "I am sorry," our host whispered. He did not have to say more. Somehow the temple priest suspected what we did in his village. Each night I packed our bags in readiness. As our host helped my father to dress, I pulled on the rest of my clothes and packed our donkey. Our host led us out a hidden gate to the village, giving us directions to the next village.

We walked until the sun was up, then stopped to drink hot tea from our flasks. My father turned his face up to the sun and smiled. "Blessed is the flame," he said. "Blessed are we who can see by its light." Then he began to cough, until he couldn't walk. In the end, I took a number of our belongings on my back, and he rode our donkey, to save his strength.

To my fear, the next village was two days' travel down the road. Snow caught us at noon, slowing us down. It was well after dark when we reached the small hut that had been set up for the wandering priesthood. By then I had been forced to give my father poppy to ease the pain of his coughing, and he was spitting up blood. Worse, when we reached the hut, I found he could not rest lying down flat. He could not breathe. The healers had warned me, had said that only a great wizard could heal him when he got this ill. I arranged our packs until he could doze sitting up. "Drink," I said, offering him a cup of the brewed medicinal tea.

My father opened his eyes.

"Mother?" he whispered, his beautiful voice only a ghost in his chest.

So I put on Omi Heza's voice for him, becoming my grandmother to give him poppy and broth, to read his favorite parts of both Books to him, until he slept. Then I sat next to him and the fire, holding his too-hot fingers to my cheek as I watched the flames.

This time I do not think I was sleeping. The flames danced for me, then pulled apart at the base to form a teardrop-shaped opening floored in embers.

The God spoke again in its twined voices. "Teky, three times we have asked, and three times you have given the wrong answer. One more chance do we give you to enter our service, to return the balance to our faithful. If you truly wish to carry on the work you have begun, what do you see?"

And there they were, tall, short, plump, dark, pale, old and young and in between, a mass of black, with eyes so bright I thought they might burn me. Last time the God had said the answer lay in my talk with Fadal. Poor Fadal, who believed the veils were chains, until I made him—her—reconsider it, briefly, at least.

I looked at those fields of women, my sisters.

"Power," I said.

The opening in the fire collapsed. I lifted my head. The heart was dark, as if something powerful had drawn the life from the fire.

The life was gone somewhere else, too. My father's hand was limp against my cheek.

Through that long night I wept and said the prayers. I rebuilt the fire to sew his shroud. The next day I built his pyre and set his spirit flying in the flames to the God we both loved. I gathered wood to replace all I had used. At last I went back inside to decide what I could do with my life.

It was nearly midnight when I remembered that my father wished me to return to my aunt.

"I don't want to go," I said aloud. The donkey snorted and glared at me.

I looked at the fire, and remembered the God had said she—he—would help me. The next village did expect a wandering priest. There had been female wandering priests before, but . . . I looked at my trembling hands: a girl's smooth young hands. Then I considered the power of the veil, and my last words to my father, spoken in my old grandmother's voice.

I had a bit of mirror in one of my packs. I scraped some ash from the hearth onto a plate, and considered the look of age.

Two days, and much practice, later, I let a young man help me up onto a platform my hosts had set for me in their barn. "Is that all right, Omi Heza?" he asked me nervously. I had wrapped myself in my grandmother's voice and name like extra veils, for strength.

I looked at a sea of male faces. It was so familiar, and yet it was not, because my father was not behind me.

"You cannot teach us!" cried some man. "You are a woman!"

"And if you were my grandson, I would give you my cane for disrespect!" I cried. Suddenly light spilled all around me, and other voices, a woman's and a man's, spoke entwined around mine. "Do you doubt I speak with the God's voice? Will you walk farther from the true flame?"

As silence spread—as the men knelt, as that dreadful light began to fade—I said in my own old-woman voice, "And bring the women and girls in here. I am too old to go on teaching once to the men and boys, and once to them. From now on, I teach all together, as the balance is meant to be."

Three days later, with a thirteen-year-old boy to be my new companion, I set forth, bound for the next village. I rode my donkey, as befitted my age.

ABOUT THE CONTRIBUTORS

JOAN BAUER was born in Oak Park, Illinois, and from her earliest memories, wanted to make people laugh. In her eight novels for young people, Joan Bauer explores difficult issues with humor and hope. Her books have won numerous awards, among them the Newbery Honor Medal, the *L.A. Times* Book Prize, the Christopher Award, and the Golden Kite Award of the Society of Children's Book Writers and illustrators. She has also been the recipient of the Michigan Thumbs-Up! Award for Children's Literature, the Delacorte Prize for a First Young-Adult Novel, the New England Booksellers Award, and the Boston Public Library's "Literary Light" Award. *Rules of the Road* was chosen as one of the top young adult books of the last twenty-five years by the American Library Association. A *New York Times* bestselling author, she lives in Brooklyn, New York. Visit her online at www.joanbaucr .com/jb.html.

CHARLES DE LINT is a full-time writer and musician who presently makes his home in Ottawa, Canada, with his wife MaryAnn Harris, an artist and musician. His most recent books are *Spirits in the Wires* and *The Blue Girl*. Other recent publications include the collections *Waifs & Strays* and *Tapping* *the Dream Tree* and *A Circle of Cats*, a picture book illustrated by Charles Vess. For more information about his work, visit his Web site at www.charlesdelint.com.

MEL GLENN was born in Switzerland, grew up in Brooklyn, served in the Peace Corps, and taught high school English for thirty-four years at his alma mater, Lincoln High School. He is the author of twelve books for young adults, including *Jump Ball*, *Foreign Exchange*, and *Who Killed Mr. Chippendale?*, which was nominated for the prestigious Edgar Allan Poe Award of the Mystery Writers of America. He has received the Christopher Award (for *Class Dismissed II*), the Golden Kite Honor Award (for *Class Dismissed*), and the American Library Association has recognized several of his titles as Best Books for Young Adults. He lives in Brooklyn with his wife, Elyse, and has two sons, Jonathan, a news writer, and Andrew, a software engineer. Since retiring, he now spends his time writing and speaking at conferences, schools, and libraries, and can be contacted at www.melglenn.com.

In the years before **PATRICE KINDL** began writing, she waited tables while attending drama school, and then became a secretary. She can now juggle six plates, lie convincingly, and type like a demon. An obsessive reader, she began writing in her late thirties. Her work has been described as: "rich and strange, haunting and humorous." Her novels have won awards, both in this country and abroad. She lives in Upstate New York with a husband, a cat, two parrots, and a Newfoundland dog. She has raised one son and two monkeys; the latter are now aides to quadriplegics. Visit her online at www.patricekindl.com.

Like the character in his story, **DAVID LUBAR** competed in magic competitions when he was young. But now he prefers to make magic on the page. He's written a wide variety of books for teens and young readers. His novel *Hidden Talents* was named a Best Book for Young Adults by the American Library Association. His other books include *Flip*, a science-fiction novel, and short-story collections *Invasion of the Road Weenies* and *In the Land of the Lawn Weenies*. He has designed and programmed a variety of video games, including *Home Alone* and *Frogger 2* for the Nintendo GameBoy, and *Fantastic Voyage* for the Atari 2600. He lives in Nazareth, Pennsylvania, with his wife, daughter, and a trio of felines. Visit him online at www .davidlubar.com.

TAMORA PIERCE is *The New York Times* and *Wall Street Journal* bestselling writer of twenty-three books of fantasy for teenagers. She was born in South Connellsville, Pennsylvania, in a long, proud line of hillbillies. While her family didn't have much money, they did have plenty of books, and books continue to be the main yardstick by which she measures true wealth. Tammy now lives in Manhattan with her beloved spouse-Creature, Web designer Tim Liebe, and their four cats and two parakeets. She hopes her books inspire her readers with the feeling that they too can do anything if they want it badly enough, and they should always follow their dreams. Visit her online at www.tamora-pierce.com.

California novelist **JOHN H. RITTER** is the recipient of the International Reading Association's Children's Book Award for *Choosing Up Sides* (1998), as well as many ALA, IRA, and state book awards for all of his work, including his highly acclaimed antiwar novel, *Over the Wall* (2000) and most recently, his best-selling magical-realism saga, *The Boy Who Saved Baseball* (2003). Known by his peers as a "writer's writer," John's lyrical prose has been singled out by booksellers and professional review journals alike as being unique among YA writers today. Visit him online at www.JohnHRitter.com.

S. L. ROTTMAN grew up in Colorado, and still considers Colorado home, even though the air force has moved her family around in recent years. While working toward her teaching certificate at Colorado State University, she received a scholarship for doing what she loves, creative writing. She wrote her first award-winning novel, *Hero*, when she was twenty-four. Because she is an avid rafter, swimmer, and football fan, sports frequently find their way into her stories. "Red Sky" is her first fantasy story.

Award-winning author **NEAL SHUSTERMAN** has published more than thirty books for young adults, including *The Schwa Was Here*, *Downsiders*, *The Dark Side of Nowhere*, and *What Daddy Did*, all of which were selected as "Best Books" by the American Library Association. *The Dark Side of Nowhere* was also selected by the American Library Association as one of the top books of the year for reluctant readers. He has won numerous state awards for his books as well, including having been on the Texas Lonestar Award list five times—most recently for his novel *Full Tilt*. As a screenwriter, Neal wrote the Disney Channel original movie *Pixel Perfect*, and his adaptation of his novel *Downsiders* is being made as an original movie for the ABC Family Channel. Neal lives in southern California with his four children.

NANCY SPRINGER has published forty-some-odd (some of them very odd) novels for children, young adults, and adults, including fantasy, mystery, contemporary fiction, and suspense. Her work has received numerous honors, including Best Adventure Book of the Year, for *Outlaw Princess of Sherwood Forest*, from *Disney Adventures* magazine in 2004, and two Edgar Allan Poe Awards from the Mystery Writers of America. *Rowan Hood Returns*, the fifth and final volume of the Rowan Hood series, was published in June, 2005. When not writing, Nancy Springer is usually to be found on a lake in a rowboat, fishing while exchanging comments with the waterfowl. Visit her online at www.stlf.org/ntc/11/nsinfo.htm.

SUZANNE FISHER STAPLES served as a news reporter and editor for United Press International for ten years in Hong Kong, India, Pakistan, Afghanistan, Bangladesh, Nepal, Sri Lanka, New York, and Washington, D.C. She later worked as a foreign news editor for *The Washington Post*. She returned to Pakistan to assess the lives of poor rural women on an assignment with the United States Agency for International Development. She is the author of *Under the Persimmon Tree*, a story about an Afghan refugee child and an American teacher, both of whom follow their stars and find each other. She also has written a memoir, *The Green Dog*, and four other novels: *Shabanu Daughter of the Wind*, a 1990 Newbery Honor book and its sequel, *Haveli*, *Dangerous Skies*, and *Shiva's Fire*, all of which have won numerous awards. She is at work on a new novel set in Pakistan, *Jameel and the House of Djinn*. She and her husband, Wayne Harley, live on a farm in rural Pennsylvania. Visit her online at www.suzannefisherstaples.com.

MICHAEL O. TUNNELL writes picture books, informational books, and novels for primary-school, middle-grade, and young-adult readers. Some of his titles include *The Children of Topaz* (1996), *Mailing May* (1997; illustrated by Ted Rand), *Brothers in Valor* (2001), *School Spirits* (1997) and his Arabian Nights novel titled *Wishing Moon* (2004). His books have received numerous awards and starred reviews and have appeared on many "best books" lists. Michael O. Tunnell teaches children's literature at Brigham Young University. He also has published several professional books, including *The Story of Ourselves: Teaching History Through Children's Literature* (1993) and *Children's Literature, Briefly* (1996), and has written articles for a variety of educational journals. He and his wife, Glenna, live in Orem, Utah. They have four grown children.

RICH WALLACE is the author of many books for teenagers, including the novels *Wrestling Sturbridge*, *Shots on Goal*, *Playing Without the Ball*, and *Restless*, and a short-story collection titled *Losing Is Not an Option*. His latest venture is a series of sports novels for younger teens called The Winning Season. He is an active participant in many sports, and lives with his wife and two sons in northeastern Pennsylvania.

SHARON DENNIS WYETH grew up in a neighborhood called Anacostia in Washington, D.C. Sharon went to college in Massachusetts. She graduated with honors from Harvard University. Sharon's childhood dream came true in 1989 when her first children's book was published. Today, she has written nearly fifty books and is also a mom. One of her favorite things is visiting schools. She also finds time for singing and weight lifting. She has been a keynote or featured speaker for organizations such as the International Reading Association and National Council of Teachers of English. She is winner of the Stephen Crane Literary Award. Visit her online at www .sharondenniswyeth.com/index.htm.

ABOUT THE EDITORS

M. JERRY WEISS is Distinguished Service Professor of Communications Emeritus, New Jersey City University. A teacher, writer, and lecturer, he has won numerous awards and honors, including the 1997 International Reading Association Special Service Award and the National Council of Teachers of English Distinguished Service Award. **HELEN S. WEISS** is an author and scholar of humor. Jerry and Helen Weiss are editors of two previous anthologies: *From One Experience to Another* and *Lost & Found*. They live in Montclair, New Jersey.